Amber's Place

Also by Gary Harmon:

The Broken Spur (a novel)

Amber's Place

Gary Allen Harmon

Drinian Press, LLC

Drinian Press/
Huron, Ohio

Drinian Press, LLC
207 Williams Street
P.O. Box 63
Huron, Ohio 44839
Visit our Web site at: www.DrinianPress.com

Library of Congress Control Number: 2019948751

ISBN-13: 978-1-941929-09-4

Printed in the United States of America

FOR DONA,

BEAUTIFUL, BRILLIANT, AND BRAVE

Author's Preface

For many years, the number of people killed in America's devastating Civil War was believed to be about 618,000. Using more modern technology, the current belief is closer to 750,000.

Further, the nation's wealth was depleted by war expenses, and wages were notoriously low if one could find employment at all. This was especially true of women.

One Baltimore sewing factory paid seamstresses less than two dollars per week. Another was reported to pay four dollars per month, a rumored figure the author believes to be true, but was unable to confirm.

Left to fend for themselves in these conditions, hundreds of American women were alone and destitute. The business of just staying alive was the marching order of the day. Of these, many would be forced to make desperate decisions that would never have been given a moment's thought in the past. Amber was one of these. Her will to survive, to do more than this, and the associations she forms along the way bring about her fall from grace and her eventual redemption.

The tale is fictional, and yet contains an abundance of true historical fact. Oceola, Haverford, and many other locations found within these pages are purely imaginary, but Amber's fictional journey could easily have been real. *Amber's Place* is indeed a historical novel in every sense of the word.

"I Love Jesus gooder'n anything. Soon's I get rich enough I'm gonna be a Christian."
Amber Juliardo, 1870

Amber's Place

Prologue

When Willet Acadia arrived in the city of Topeka, it only took a moment for him to be glad he lived in Oceola. Large towns and cities were decidedly not his cup of tea. Noisy traffic and the profusion of daily activities went hand in hand with cities like Topeka and Kansas City. Willet had visited both and liked neither.

It was not much trouble to find the offices of Mid-West Land Development Inc. Their sign was bright blue letters on a field of snowy white and hung above the door and just below another sign that said: THE PARKER BUILDING. The construction was a five-story affair that was an excellent example of what modern architects believed neoclassic revival architecture looked like.

A pale limestone façade with a myriad of Corinthian columns, broken pediments, dentils, and a sunburst tympanum above the entrance gave the impression of someone who tried, but too hard. Upon entering the spacious interior, he was surprised to learn the Mid-West company occupied the entire first floor. Black, felt spaghetti boards with white press on letters identified the various departments that made up the complex.

One read: HOME LOANS. Another said: TAX ABATEMENT AND HOMESTEAD. Yet another announced: FORECLOSURES FOR SALE. Willet approached a pretty young woman sitting at a large mahogany desk covered in telephones and file folders. Her auburn hair hung in springy ringlets around her lovely face. Willet thought her hair— though not quite as deep-red—resembled his Irish Setter, O'Malley. A different shade of red perhaps, but the curls were the same.

"I have an appointment with Mister Ashby," he told her.

"Cary or Rob?" she queried.

"I'm not sure. I didn't know there were two. It's about some land I'm offering for sale."

"Acquisition," she offered. "Straight down to the end of the mall; it's on the right. I'll buzz him and let him know you're coming. It's Rob, by the way."

Rob Ashby turned out to be a tall, rather angular man with thick glasses and a firm handshake.

"I've been expecting you, Mister Acadia. We sent our team out to Oceola and they found your parcel. I believe you told me it was sixteen acres. Isn't that right?"

"Yeah. Just a shade over."

"I found the abstract so interesting. It was like a history lesson," Ashby smiled.

"I guess you know more about it than I do."

"A lot of history has been lost of course. Prior to the civil war, your parcel was part of a land claim of more than two thousand acres."

Willet gasped a bit. "Was it legal to claim that much?" he asked.

"Not really. But enterprising homesteaders from that period would make a claim for as much as they could. Then they'd throw up a building—sometimes just a shack. Claim that as an improvement and claim the same amount of adjoining land. Then do it again and again. Not much checking in those days. Land like this was really in the boonies. Didn't have much value either. We covet prairie lands. Our ancestors, not so much."

"But all that acreage, what happened to it?"

"Going through the abstract of recorded sales, I counted fourteen. That doesn't consider those that were never recorded. The earliest recorded title I found was Christof Romero. Then Charlotte Romero. Now that's strange."

"Why so?"

"I'm not sure women were allowed to hold property in their name at that time. Anyway, a lot of other names follow. It takes a long time to get to your name, Acadia. But let's talk about the parcel we're interested in. And we are interested. Just a matter of getting the terms agreeable to both of us.

The property has a couple of serious problems. At least serious for us."

"And what are they?" Willet wanted to know.

"Well, the old cemetery for one. We won't build atop a gravesite. There's no real law against it. Especially when they have been deserted for a hundred years or more, as is the case in point—except the law of morality, of course. We have a company law. We just don't do it.

"When our firm was new, we did it a time or two and ended up paying so many legal bills we could have afforded to raise the Titanic. So, no. If we buy your property, we'll build a four-foot stone or brick wall completely around it. We'll clean up the site and perhaps landscape it. It's only a half an acre but we won't build within two hundred feet of it.

"Now we're talking about thirteen and three quarters acres. The homes we think that are right for that location will be about fourteen hundred square feet. Four bedroom, two bath, and attached two car garage. A house like that should sell for one hundred thirty-nine to a hundred and sixty-four thousand. It should also require at least a half of an acre lot size. Taking in consideration of our streets, sidewalks, and a bit of green space, we see ten...maybe twelve homes here. Then there's the matter of the old mansion."

"Yeah. No one has lived there in a long time. Probably not in sixty or seventy years."

"The thing we have to watch out for—and believe me it happens more often than you think— as soon as we start to raze the house, some local group is going to decide it's a historic property and of cultural value. Some old house guild will claim it's of historical value and stop us in our tracks."

"No one has ever shown any interest in the old place. I doubt it would happen." Willet scratched his chin thoughtfully. "If it were to happen, would there be any way around it?"

"Sure. Just restore it. Put one of those bronze plaques out in front and open it up for tourists. Not that any tourist would ever visit it. Too bad the old place never just caught fire. This transaction would be an easy one then."

"Mister Ashby, are you suggesting I torch the old place?"

"Oh no! Certainly not. We would never advocate an act like that. But please understand. With that old house in place, it seriously affects the strength of our offer. Why don't you just go back home and look the old place over. You're married, I assume?"

"Yes."

"Talk it over with your wife. I don't think it wise to talk to neighbors about it, but do what you want. I think my firm could see two hundred thousand or even two hundred twenty-five thousand dollars if the house were gone."

"And if the house stayed?"

"I would have to see if our main office would have any further interest, Mister Acadia. Our interest is building homes. Twelve miles from what we call the subject property, there are twenty-four thousand full and part time employees building Lear aircraft. Kansas is now number two in wind-produced energy. That's an industry that hasn't even started to grow yet, and as long as there is a prairie, there's going to be wind. Kansas is still rich in agriculture, but we're not just a farm state anymore. We want to give some of these folks a place to live."

"I see."

"Go on home and think about it, Mister Acadia. I was planning to come to Oceola next week to look the property over for a final observation. We can see where we stand then. Fair enough?"

"Yes. I suppose so. I think that's best really. Wife and I need a day or so. Next week is fine."

When Willet left the office of Rob Ashby, his head was spinning. His father, Adam Acadia, had never wanted to sell the old place at all. The taxes weren't much. It didn't cost much just to keep it. Did he really want to sell? He knew the land had been in his family at least four generations. Maybe more.

Who was Charlotte Romero? Was he her descendant? Did he really want to sell to Rob Ashby? What would Jennifer say? There were a lot of things that interested Jennifer more than money. Rob Ashby had spoken of an old house guild perhaps posing a problem. When he thought about it, it seemed Jennifer was exactly the kind of person that would find importance in such an organization.

As he steered his Buick home, he spotted a private plane ahead of and above him. "Learjet," he said to himself. Rob Ashby had given him more information than he was probably supposed to. He wondered if a week would be enough. He had owned the property nearly ten years, ever since his father's death.

Maybe it's time I looked into it a little more, he thought.

Chapter One

Oceola, Kansas 1884

The Oceola train yard was as dark as Grady Cole could have ever imagined. Hand over hand, he gingerly felt his way among the dozens of sided freight cars. Only a few stars in the Kansas sky afforded any light whatsoever, and Grady found comfort in the heft of the rifle in his hands. Suddenly, fifty yards ahead the flicker and flare of a lighted match alerted him. In a moment, it was gone. It had lasted only long enough to serve as the warning he needed. He levered a live round into the chamber of the Winchester.

It was as he had expected. The news of such a rich cargo sitting in the freight yards of the Atchison, Topeka and Santa Fe was just too tempting to the likes of Alton Starret and his little weasel of a handyman, Billy Whitsell. The story circulating around the town of Oceola of a hundred thousand dollars resting in the mail car of a train just setting in the freight yards was more than Starret and Whitsell could resist. After nearly a lifetime of stealing pitiful hauls of loot, the promise of this kind of a payoff was not to be ignored.

Harder to understand were the posters scattered about town offering a five-hundred-dollar reward for the arrest of Alton Starret. For an outlaw with such a low standing to have a cash bounty on his head was exceedingly mysterious. As fate would turn the trick, Starret had caused the problem when he held up a jitney coach just north of Oceola.

These little jitney runs were short trips, usually by buckboard, buggy, or sometimes by one of the old reconditioned stagecoaches that carried passengers to nearby destinations where a trains were not an option. A towheaded youngster of eight or nine called Pauly Eugene once asked his mother why the ride was called a *jitney*. She replied, "That's what the old folks used to call a nickel. The rides cost more than that, but they's only worth 'bout a nickel."

After some thought, and many times thereafter, Pauly could be heard asking, "Momma, can I have a jitney?"

A robbery such as this would likely yield only the watch or cash of the passengers. There would be no plunder of the jitney driver who was well aware that he should carry nothing of value. Also, it was known these journey-for-fare drivers generally went unarmed. The prize just was not enough to die for.

This little holdup staged by Starret would likely have attracted little attention, if only Millicent Gable was not on the coach that day. She was the beloved daughter of Winston Gable of the First National People of Kansas Bank. The whole thing would not have been so important if one of his own daughters had not been a passenger on that particular day, on that particular coach. The reward was posted by Winston Gable, who was so outraged he wanted to add the legend "Dead or Alive". Marshal Cole had forbidden that inclusion.

Hearing his robbery had attracted a reward gave Alton Starret a feeling of prominence he had not experienced heretofore. It also emboldened him beyond measure. When he heard talk of real money sitting in the rail yard, he saw himself with his new stature of grandeur and knew he had to try for it. Whitsell was so impressed with a reward being offered for his pal, it was no trick to have him eagerly join right in.

There was no money. The rumor of the wealth awaiting the one daring enough to take it was a ruse. A trap created by Grady Cole himself. Cole knew an outlaw of any stature would recognize the ruse at once and he had relied upon Starret's ineptness to lure him into the net.

He's here! He's taken the bait! A little luck, the marshal thought to himself, "I only need a little luck to clean this mess up."

As dull as they were, Starret and Whitsell had somehow outwitted and outrun Federal Marshal Grady Cole, for no less than five months in the late summer and early fall, and now Grady felt it was about to end, one way or another. He felt a tight knot low in his stomach, and his mouth tasted of old iron. He crept closer to the outlaw pair and waited for the inevitable light.

It was just as dark for the bandits as it was for him, and he realized that in order to enter the mail car and move strongboxes, they would at some point be forced to strike a lantern. Once they were in the light, no matter how faint, and he was cloaked by a mantle of dark, it would be all the edge he needed, or was likely ever to get.

Thinking it out, he recognized that the minute he called for them to surrender, they would instantly extinguish whatever light they had and make off into the darkness. Also, in the dark he was no safer than they were.

This was a decision he hesitated to make. In his thirty years as a peace officer, he had never shot a man, any man, if he could detect another way. Never had he ambushed an unsuspecting felon although many peace officers of that era were masters of the "bushwhack arrest." Here in this ebony gloom, he knew there was no other way. His best option was to disable the one with the light with a shot from the Winchester. He would try to disable and not to kill, but, in this light, whatever happened would be in the hands of a higher authority than himself.

He hoped that when one outlaw saw the other fall, and he called out for a surrender, it would end there. And since there were no reports of either Whitsell or Starret ever being involved in a shooting, he thought the chances were somewhat favorable. If he could end up with a prisoner and a wounded hostage, it would be all he could ask for.

He crept closer to the pair. He was so near now he could hear their muffled whispers and the scuffle of their boots on the graveled yard. Shouldering the rifle now, he waited, the muzzle pointing off into the dark in the general direction of the faint sounds he was fixing on. He knew the lighted lantern had to come. No one could work in this gloom.

Suddenly there it was–the spark and then the flare of a match. He could see the slow growth of the tiny kerosene fire ball within the lantern and the slow spread of the amber glow lighting the faces of the two men kneeling on the blind stoop. They were bent over the lock on the mail car door.

In a moment, the quiet of the Kansas blackness was shattered by the explosive bark of the 44-40 Winchester. Someone audibly gasped in the darkness and the lantern fell, shattering itself on the tailgate floor. Almost immediately, the spreading kerosene ignited, bringing a bright radiance to the stygian darkness.

"Hands up, you sumbitches!" he called out. One man was all he could see. He was standing well back, lighted by the burning kerosene. He reasoned the man he had shot had fallen from the freight car and into the darkness.

"Is that you, Grady?" the standing man called back. "That you, you old bushwhacker, you?"

"Federal Marshal here! Get them hands up, or I'll shoot!"

"Shoot away, you old bastard—and here's a little somethin' for ya!"

In the faint amber glow of the spilt kerosene, Grady saw the standing man suddenly produce a pistol and point the gun in the direction of the voice he had just heard. Without any way of aiming, he fired a rapid two shots at the area he determined to be the source of the voice. These potshots were answered by two hurried blasts from the Winchester and then a fusillade of pistol reports as the bandit emptied his pistol into the darkness.

-oOo-

It was nearly eleven o'clock in the gentle October evening as Emmett Poindexter took his old beagle hound, Smarty, for his evening relieving walk just as he did every evening for more than ten years. This night was especially dark, but Emmett and Smarty had trod this path so often the darkness was no hindrance for them.

Both Emmett and his dog were enjoying the quiet stroll when out of the Kansas night a multitude of gunshots jolted them. Smarty, always being a bit gun shy, leapt to one side and tugged mightily on his leash.

"What in hell is that, Smarty? Is them gunshots? Who's adoin' all that shootin'? Sounds like in the freight yard, don't you think?" He felt foolish as he realized he was awaiting an answer from his dog. Halted now, Emmett and Smarty waited. Silence returned to the blanket of night above Oceola.

Emmett diligently waited and listened for more gunfire, or whatever those explosions were. After a while, he told himself it was over.

"Wonder what was that?" he asked Smarty. Smarty was silent. Standing alert in the darkness, Emmett Poindexter and his dog listened intently for more explosions. What they heard was the faint whistle of a whippoorwill. A sound that all from Kansas knew and loved.

Chapter Two

Haverford, Kansas

Life with Oney and Maude Ledbetter was all I had ever known. And as I look back on it, it was a pretty good life at that. Living on the small Ledbetter ranch was a fine and exciting life for a boy. There was a small cow herd of Herefords so there was the calving to look forward to each spring. Chickens were constantly underfoot, as were a pair of belligerent goats. I had a fine pony to ride, and our creek boasted some of the biggest catfish in Caroll county.

Oney Ledbetter was a lean and gentle man given to wearing bib overalls and sturdy work shoes. Many ranchers of the area dressed in riding clothes, boots, and Stetson hats. Oney, in comparison, appeared rather plain, I suppose, in his high-top work shoes and striped railroader's cap. But to me, he was the grandest man on earth.

I learned everything from Papa Oney. To ride, throw a rope, castrate, dehorn, and midwife birthing cows and heifers, and all the things that a cowman must know. He was a gentle teacher, with a love for the cattle he stewarded, as well as the very land that was such a part of him. These were all things of enormous importance, and that I would never forget. But mostly I prized it when he spoke of horses. The horse and the crafts of horsemanship were nearly a religion for him.

When Papa Oney had been a very young man, and before he had followed the wagon trails to the west, when he still was a Kentuckian, he had lived and worked amid the great racehorse farms of Lexington and Louisville. A young man mucking stalls at first, his aptitude and his willingness to learn had soon elevated him, first, to exercise boy, and then, at last, to assistant trainer and subservient to the veterinarians who cared for these precious animals.

When I think of Maude Ledbetter, I feel a warmth in my heart. I could not have had a mother who loved and cared for me with more diligence than this fine lady. Papa said she was the one that named me. Woody's my name. Well it's really Woodrow, but everybody just says Woody. Maude says it was my real Momma who really named me. Papa Oney said she's dead now, and she was real pretty. I 'spect she's an angel now. I don't know how I can miss her so much since I never remember seeing her. But I do. I used to think that when I see her up in heaven, I got a lot of things I'm going to ask her.

Unlike Papa Oney though, Momma Maude was the wild colt of the prairie. "Spring steel and gunpowder," Papa Oney would say as he described her. "You mess with Maudy," he was often heard to say, "She'll kick a slat out of yer wagon!" Politics was Maude's favorite subject to excite herself about. Of course, the nation electing Grover Cleveland for a second term gave her more to rage about than ever before. Who could blame her? These were, after all, the years of near worship of the most popular of all presidents heretofore. Abraham Lincoln was all but a God to many Americans, save the deep south.

He had carved the way for a new party called the Republicans, and they had held sway until the appearance of one, Grover Cleveland, and the first Democrat electee for many years. Not only did this pretentious lawyer bring about the success of his party once, he would lay out a term, and then be re-elected to become the only American president to serve two nonconsecutive terms. It was more than any self-respecting Republican could abide.

Cleveland's strongest plank in the platform was his belief that the government should keep its nose from the people's business. Maude took this as an excuse for the government to avoid doing anything at all for the people. This was still solidly within the restoration period of the civil war, and many citizens, friends of ours, simply had nothing.

Momma Maude's way of thinking was the people needed help, and if the government didn't help her own people, why did it exist at all.

Aside from Momma Maude's fiery speeches about right and wrong, I recall her wonderful cooking. The fare was plain indeed, but prepared in a way I couldn't wait to get to the table.

Wonderful beef roasts drenched in brown drippings. Succulent fried chicken with cornbread and cream gravy. Sourdough biscuits with our own home smoked ham or bacon for breakfast. Stewed apples and hot Arbuckle's chicory coffee laced with the fresh thick cream from our little Jersey cow, Jennifer. I could go on about this subject, but I'm not sure I could find a place to stop.

About my background, and how I came to be adopted by these fine folks, very little was ever said. Just that an angel had brought me to their door when I was a baby.

I was told often that someday my father would come to get me. About my mother nothing was ever offered. I thought about my real father a lot. *Who was he?* I wondered. *What was he like? Would he be as good to me as Papa Oney?*

I wasn't all that sure I wanted my father to show up and take me away from the Ledbetter's. Still I pondered often. Especially at night. I would lay in my warm feather bed and stare at the moon from the window of my little upstairs room and wonder if my father could be looking at the moon the same as me. At the same time.

Sometimes, maybe once a month, Papa Oney would hitch the team of Percherons to the flat wagon. He and Momma Maude would perch themselves on the high spring seat, and I would sit cross-legged on the wagon's flat bed with my dog, Bones, and we would ride the six miles to the little town of Haverford.

I loved these trips more than I could ever say. First of all, the big Percheron team was so magnificent, that everyone we would pass by on the dirt road to town would marvel at their beauty. There were not likely many folks we were to meet along the way, but the ones we did encounter showered us with compliments about the appearance of our team.

Dappled grey as they were, and looking so wonderful in their oiled harnesses, most folks called them *circus* horses. And indeed, they did seem to be the favorite breed of bareback and trick riders. I had seen them on colorful posters that told when there was to be a circus somewhere in the area. I longed that one day I would see a circus for myself. To see the Percherons perform! What sheer joy that would be.

There were many other things that I loved about that little trip, too. Just a dirt road and hardly even a house along the way. Just the McCutcheon farm and the old Wallace shack. It was truly a trip through a wild and primitive land.

The pronghorn antelope stood along the roadside and stared at us as we passed along the way. Almost every trip, we'd encounter a big old diamondback rattler sunning himself in the dust of the lane. The Percheron team hated these snakes and would really act up when they spotted one. Papa Oney would leave the wagon and using the butt of his whip he'd lift the rattler and move him to the roadside.

He'd stand by the team cooing and caressing their faces, talking baby talk to them until they were calm again. Most other folks always killed snakes when they came upon them. Papa Oney never killed a snake, I'd guess. Least wise when I was there.

Wild horses would be seen once in a while, but they were so shy a glimpse of them was a special treat. Of course, coyotes were ever present, and once we got a fleeting glance at a bobcat. These trips were rare and wonderful when I was twelve.

The six mile trip took about three hours, and Momma Maude would bring along cold ham and biscuits, along with a stone jar of buttermilk. Sometimes she'd fry up a chicken or a cottontail that

I had shot that very morning. On a sunny Kansas day, these voyages were pleasures never to be forgotten.

And then, of course, there was the town itself. One of my most vivid recollections was the giant tooth. It hung there, just as you entered the town, on a chain about ten feet up in the air. A tooth as big as a wagon wheel. Someone said it was a molar, I think. I thought it was wonderful. Its purpose, of course, was to advertise the services of Doctor Roland Rhinehart, the town dentist.

There were other attractions that appealed to me, to be sure. I loved it when we passed the blacksmith's shop. You could smell the acrid smoke of the charcoal and hear the ring of Mr. Gesselman's hammer against the anvil as he shaped horseshoes from iron heated till it glowed cherry red.

A special thing happened when he pulled the cord that fed the bellows into the forge. It would blow a massive shower of sparks hurtling skyward in a fiery explosion. It was like the Fourth of July. It must be wonderful to be a blacksmith. To work amid that smoke and showering sparks and glowing metal, and to actually make something from iron, I thought. It must be a work to make a man proud. Far better than being a dentist for a life's work, I supposed.

I could not help but remember Mr. Wallace. An old man who came to buy eggs from Momma Ledbetter from time to time. When he grinned at me, which was often, I could see his teeth. A grim portion of blackened, rotted snags. When I thought of that sight, I could feel the bile rise into my throat nearly gagging me. When I recalled Mr. Wallace, I was sure being a dentist was not for me. I'd bet if Doctor Rhinehart ever saw Ethan Wallace, he'd ponder on becoming a blacksmith.

But the best treat of all was to visit Hiram Watkins. Hiram was about two years older than me. He had red hair and bunches of freckles and worked in the livery stable. Hands down, Hiram was the smartest fellow I'd ever met. Hiram knew all about most everything. The time I spent with him taught me more than I had ever learned in Mrs. Brandley's one-room schoolhouse.

Hiram knew all about girls and where babies came from. He could play a guitar and just sing like anything. Once he tried to show me how to roll a cigarette. He could roll a smoke so tight it wouldn't hardly draw. I never learned to do anything but crumple the paper and spill the tobacco. I didn't really want to smoke anyhow. Once, when I asked Papa Oney could I try his pipe, he said I could if I really wanted to, but he wished I'd wait till I was fifteen. Papa Oney never asked for much from me. I figured it was alright to wait.

Best thing ever was a trip to McCandless' store. It was true. We had barber pole candy. We had big old jawbreakers that took near all day to eat. We had peach soda pop in glass bottles that really popped when you pried the stopper loose. Momma Maude always saw to it that I had a dime or two and that was plenty.

The neighbor farm to our place was Mr. and Mrs. McCutcheon. They had the prettiest daughter in all of Crawford County, Ida Mae McCutcheon. Momma Maude would always buy a little sack of candy for us to give Ida Mae when we passed her farm on the way home. Sometimes I'd leave the wagon and visit with her, and play on her oak tree swing, and walk the rest of the way home about dark.

I told Momma Maude I wanted to give Ida Mae the candy, and I wanted to tell her some of the things I'd heard from Hiram. Momma got real mad. She said if I said anything to Ida Mae I had heard from Hiram Watkins, she'd wallop me good. Momma had never walloped me before, but she was so mad this time I thought she might.

She said Hiram was full of sheep dip. We gave Ida Mae the candy on the way home, but Papa Oney said it would be better if I stayed in the wagon. I wasn't allowed to see Ida Mae for a long time after that.

The visit to town near my twelfth birthday was one I'll never forget. That was the trip when Papa Oney took me to Ashby's hardware store and bought me the twenty-two rifle. My own gun! I recall that gun even today. I can see it in my mind's eye as clearly as ever.

A beautiful blue steel octagon barrel. Smooth walnut wood made the perfect stock. The little under lever that dropped the breech block so I could insert the single twenty-two caliber shell. "Crack Shot" was engraved on the top of the barrel. It was the finest treasure I had ever received. Made even more valuable, as I look back, because it was a gift from Papa and Momma Ledbetter. So dear to me.

I won't forget that wagon ride home from that trip. Admiring my wonderful rifle, I was already making plans to own other guns someday. "Someday, Papa, I want to have a pistol," I announced.

I recall Papa's answer. "Pistols are trouble, son. They're not made for hunting squirrels and rabbits. Stay with your rifle. It'll do more than any pistol, and it's not as likely to cause troubles."

Momma Ledbetter added, "We had a pistol once. That's how we came to leave Kentucky. I'd ask you to promise me you'd never have a pistol. I'd ask you to, but I know you won't make that promise. And if you did, you wouldn't keep it."

Being a boy that loved his Momma, I quickly answered, "It's okay, Momma. I promise." But I wondered about Kentucky.

Two days after that memorable trip, I was stunned when Papa Oney told me that my father was coming to visit, and that he might want me to go away with him. He was to arrive in about a week. It was the longest week I'll ever recollect.

Chapter Three

Amber Juliardo stood in front of her full-length mirror in her first-floor bedroom in the Twin Oaks Manor house in a mood of self-appraisal. She had to admit she approved. She had maintained her svelte appearance and, in her opinion, looked somewhat younger than her genuine years. At thirty-seven, she was indeed a handsome woman. More than handsome, she was successful. She had set herself a goal and had succeeded.

Not only was the big white house with the green shutters, known as Twin Oaks in deference to the pair of magnificent oak trees that flanked the graveled lane that was the entry way to the fine old house, hers, bought and paid for—mortgage-free, it was also the most successful bordello within fifty miles of Oceola, Kansas.

Madam Amber, while not exactly rich, could certainly be categorized as *quite well off*. It had taken more years than she wanted to remember, but the last two had been the culmination of hard work and mostly diligence.

She was glad that the sweaty and gritty work that brought her here was over, but she knew that it had to happen in order to work the plan. Her plan to eventually run a house of her own had run afoul of male intervention far more times than she cared to remember. *For some inexplicable reason,* she thought to herself, *men think they should run this business when it's obviously the world of a woman.* Pensive now, she thought back to the start of the long journey that had brought her to this point:

New Orleans, 1872

At any one time, there likely would be more than a dozen girls working the space between Bourbon and Basin Streets. On New Orleans' lower side, near the docks, were as many. These though, were the lower-class street walkers, seeking out the residues of the city. Any man in the dock area after dark was likely to be a grifter, cut purse, or thief and likely dangerous.

Amber's beauty served her quite well on the corner of Basin Street near the Captains' Court Tavern. As walkers went, she was as successful as the best. Still, she knew there had to be a better way to conduct her trade. Especially as she watched her sisters in trade turn over most of the money they earned to some man, who had either convinced them that they needed his acumen and guidance in conducting their commerce, or they were so terrified they willingly acquiesced. She knew then that these girls squandered what little was left for liquor or cocaine to enable themselves to make it through one more day. Amber knew they would end up with nothing. She vowed it would not be her way.

Amber herself was set upon nightly by these brigands who called themselves *Whoremasters*. Each had a different tale as to why she should become a "Pony" in their stable. Nightly, she resisted by laughing them off or telling them that she was already in a stable. Then she sensed it was becoming dangerous.

Some of the other street girls began pointing her out to their male bullies, and questioning that if she needed no services from a Whoremaster, why then should they? Amber realized that this was becoming a hazard to her work, and perhaps even to her life. She sensed she was causing too much trouble. It was bound to boil over soon.

It was one of her evenings spent with Daniel Ricardo that was about to change things for her. Even to influencing her future. Ricardo was one of Amber's regular customers, and she sometimes saw him as often as twice a week. He was not one to hurry her to her hotel room to expedite his urgency, but rather he always insisted on taking her somewhere.

Sometimes to a nice dinner. A play or concert. Amber appreciated this very unusual treatment, but at the same time it took her off the street and interfered with her earnings. Daniel, though, was glad to pay her extra for her accompaniment. While Amber thought it an extravagance, she was happy to go along with it. She liked Daniel Ricardo and he took her interesting places. He was also respectful of her in the bedroom and made no distasteful demands. Hands down, he was her favorite date of the moment.

It was on a hot August night that he suggested they take a carriage down to the tenderloin of Orleans. He told her of the bare-knuckle boxing matches held on Saturday nights on one of the wharfs. It sounded awful to Amber, but Daniel convinced her she might enjoy it. There would be gambling of course, and he would cover a few bets for her. "It will be an evening of great sport," he told her.

At least, she thought, *a carriage ride would be pleasant and perhaps cooler than my room.*

As soon as she observed the crowd gathered at Wharf Three, she felt the hair on the back of her neck bristle. It was unlike any gathering she had seen before. Here were men dressed in regal finery. Others dressed in the garb of tradesmen and seafarers. Beautiful ladies in gowns that cost what Amber would earn in a year. Black men in top hats and cutaway coats. Cajun royalty in silk and brocade.

The ring was a square of sorts bounded by hawser line from some nearby ship. The glow of dozens of flaming torches lighted the area and gave the scene a look of some grim celebration. A carnival or a funeral? Amber could not decide which. Amber felt a stir in her stomach as the first two opponents took the ring.

Naked save the loin cloth each wore about their middle, the two men were spectacular in size and musculature. An announcer told the crowd the way the bout would be conducted and gave the names of each of the battlers. Someone struck a bucket with a metal dipper and the two left their corners and moved to the center of the ring. In less than two minutes, the larger man with the long blond hair was battered unconscious and lay flat on his back on the plank floor of the makeshift arena.

Blood streamed from the fallen warrior's mouth and nose. The victor raised his arms to celebrate his speedy triumph. Amber felt herself being at once repulsed and unexplainably attracted to the gory spectacle. She had never seen anything so stirring as the two magnificent stallions locked in the primitive embrace of deadly combat. As repulsed as she might be, she knew she would see more of this marvel. It was horrible and equally irresistible.

The crowd of spectators was aroar as men shuffled to and fro, jostling each other, and collecting their wagers or paying them off. It was during this melee of gamblers handling their business that the next two combatants came into view. Amber was shaken to realize she had seen one of the men before. A giant of a man, fierce looking with his shaved head and broad mustache, he entered the ring with an air of confidence almost to the point of arrogance. Amber searched her memory. She knew she had seen this man before, but where? She just couldn't put her finger on the circumstance.

Broad of shoulder, his huge body tapered to a muscular waist. Held aloft on powerful legs, this fighter was the most magnificent man Amber had ever seen. She thought, "Mighty. Mighty would be an apt description for him." She labored trying to recall where she had seen him before.

The announcer was instructing the crowd again, and then she heard his name. "Antoine Acadia," the announcer called out. In a flash, hearing his name it came back to her. "Tracy's!" she said almost aloud, "Tracy's Bistro—West Bourbon Street!" Antoine Acadia was a bar man at Tracy's!

She first saw him one evening when her business was unusually slow. She had walked further west on Bourbon Street than she ever had before.

Eventually she found herself standing in front of a small bistro that bore the name *Tracy's* painted in old script letters on the glass of the window. She wondered why she had never heard of this place.

Ordinarily she knew every public room on Bourbon Street. A bit tired from the long walk, she opted for a spot of coffee and so she entered Tracy's. It was a dimly lit room consisting of a long bar and an assortment of tables. All occupied by men. She knew at once why the place was foreign to her. This was a social house where men came to meet other men. And as he was pouring wine into delicate glasses from a large decanter, she had first laid eyes on Antoine Acadia. And now she found herself beholding at him again.

All of her life she had been led to believe that these men who were attracted to sex with other men were weak, feminine, and girlish. The battle she saw this particular evening disproved a goodly amount of that. Antoine Acadia proved to be the most brutal person she had ever encountered.

Indeed, she believed that she had met her share of toughs on the New Orleans streets and near her seedy wharf. Amber had seen nothing like this. Antoine had crushed his opponent in a short three minutes but continued to batter him bloody and senseless. When the seconds tried to halt the battle and award Antoine the victory, he smashed into them with the same velocity he had dealt his challenger.

She found herself somehow inexplicably drawn to this savage onslaught and found herself sizing up this most ruthless combatant. In his near nudity he somehow strangely excited her. She estimated he was a few inches taller than six feet. Perhaps six three or four. His weight could have been anywhere from two hundred twenty-five pounds up to two fifty.

Whatever he was, she knew strength when she saw it. He had arms heavily corded with ropy sinew, broad shoulders tapering to a narrow waist of gathered muscle, and bare legs that were oaken trunks. She felt herself attracted to this strange and beautiful being. But when she allowed herself to imagine Antoine Acadia being more than friends with another man, she felt perplexed and a little sad.

The next week was a whirlwind of the strangest happenings for Amber. Daniel had insisted on seeing her every evening. Each evening he would call for her at her rooms and escort her to the best places the night had to offer. She instinctively knew something was about to happen. That Daniel was leading up to something. She thought she might know what it was, and she hoped she was wrong.

It was in an exotic saloon called *Lady Godiva's Bistro* that her fear was realized. After two drinks apiece of the potent little aperitif called absinth, Daniel took Amber's hand gently in his own, and looking deeply into her eyes, and in his most sincere tone asked her to marry him. It was precisely that which she had feared.

"My, you certainly give a girl something to think about," she crooned. "I'll need a moment to settle myself Daniel. I'm a bit overcome. I need a moment in the powder room."

"Can't you give me your answer, Amber?" he implored.

"Please, a little patience darling. My heart's aflutter right now. I'll have an answer the moment I'm back. I think you already know what the answer will be," she teased him with an extravagant smile. She excused herself and left the table.

"Don't be too long, sweetheart," Daniel chided, "I'm looking forward to beginning a new life with you."

Amber walked directly to the rear of the room, but instead of entering the ladies powder room, she instead slipped out a back door into the dark alley behind the bistro and disappeared into the blackness of the New Orleans' night.

It had happened once before. A sailor from the wharf area had also asked her to marry. Both the sailor and now Daniel had proposed marriage with not a word spoken about her curtailing her nighttime streetwalking. Amber had seen this before. It happened to girls of the night all too often, and Amber vowed she would not let it happen to her.

These proposals did not come from suitors wanting a wife. Amber knew exactly what they wanted. It was to be her pimp. To share in the money she earned with her body. Not to become husbands—rather *whoremasters*! Amber went back to her little rooms and cried the rest of the night.

The next week proved to be the most trying Amber could recall. She would be robbed three times that week. Once by a pair of young black men who pushed her to the ground and took her bundle of ointments that her profession required from time to time.

Next, her assailant was a sailor who tore her dress and terrified her with a dagger held to her throat. He took nothing but left her shaking with fear and realizing what a dangerous position she was in. Finally, a trio of other walking girls again took her bundle of goods and pushed her down on the cobblestones.

With this last attack, her suspicions were confirmed. These were all attacks orchestrated by her former lover, Daniel, Daniel Ricardo. She knew the assaults would continue until she submitted. Perhaps eventually they would even kill her.

Daniel's reach was longer than hers and his assistants were stronger.

She realized she needed protection from these onslaughts, but who? Who would champion her? Surely not the police. They were far more likely to arrest her than aid her. The thought of six months or a year in a jute mill was not what she needed. The other women of the street might have aided her if not so terrified themselves.

"I need help," she cried to herself, "I need someone stronger—ruthless—maybe even willing to kill." And then the thought crossed her mind like a lightning flash, "I need Antoine, Antoine Acadia."

Chapter Four

The House of Mendoza, Acadia, Spain

In the Year of Our Lord 1294, Alphonse Herrera stood bewildered yet enormously grateful as he gazed at the long sloping hillside. A lovely inclined meadow sweeping down to the spring fed lake that had recently been gifted to him by Queen Maria de Molina, bride of King Sancho el Bravo. A royal boon afforded him as reward for his valiant service and his grievous wounds suffered in the last big battle of the final wars of Christ.

There had been eighty such wars over the past three hundred years since. They came about as Holy Father Pope Urban had commanded all of Christendom to take the Holy Land and any relic pertaining to Jesus of Nazareth or the Holy Bible away from the Muslim populace, who had held these treasures since the Roman government of all of Palestine and Judea, along with other regions that could be termed Holy Lands, had been vanquished.

Surprisingly, some of these ancient relics, and particularly the cities, were as important to Muslim traditions as to the Catholic. And so, war. The valiant knights and princes of all of Europe, including Portugal and Spain had gathered their armies, some as far away from the Holy Land as three thousand miles, and marched on the Middle East as a punitive force to reckon with the infidel.

Battle after bloody battle, the balance of power constantly shifting, the European legions, after three centuries, at last realized it was time to return to their homes. What they found horrified them. Three hundred years of the constant extravagances of a foreign war, coupled with an absence of management of the national commerce, had plunged their once affluent nations into abject poverty. These bold and heroic warlords returned to find the people who had supported the effort of the Crusades with their very being were now destitute, starving, and clothed in rags.

Alphonse Herrera, never of royalty, had enlisted as an archer as many young men had. Willing to die for love of Jesus, and anxious to punish the Muslim factors for their unbelief, they had found themselves in a far bloodier and far less holy struggle than they could have conceived. Seeking the glories of a conquering legion, they found instead heat, sand, starvation and, all too often, defeat at the hands of the squads of Saladin, mounted on their splendid Arabian chargers.

The last of these fights, victory having belonged to the Muslim force, sent Herrera along with a fighting force of eighty men on the start of their two-year long march home. At last arriving at their homeland and about to start into the overwhelming task of rebuilding their lives, they were suddenly called, by royal command from no less than Queen Maria de Molina herself, to muster under the royal chapel of the Basilica in the royal Pantheon, the honored place of burial for the kings of Spain.

Of the eighty that had begun, six were left from the brutal ordeal of the march afoot to reach their homelands on the Iberian Peninsula. The little ragged and confused cadre appeared at the Basilica as ordered, each having no idea what to expect. The royal lady herself warmly thanked each of the warriors for their valiant service to Lord Jesus, and each man was awarded a leather bag of golden coin as big as a man's fist.

But when she saw her soldier Alphonse, had covered his face with a kerchief, she halted in front of him. "Sir Warrior, I beg of you remove your mask that I might see the countenance of such a valiant servant of our Lord." Alphonse shook his head and tried his best to refuse her request. Persistent, she at last commanded the mask's removal.

Now gazing upon her countryman's face, she was at once horrified and heartbroken. The slash from the mounted Saracen's scimitar had claimed Herrera's nose and upper lip. Queen Maria was staring at a face that once was as human as her own, but now was only an expression of horror. A ghastly apparition made up of eyes and teeth.

"Re-cover your face, good sir," she exclaimed. Then commanding five of her soldiers to have their gold and be on their way with her blessing, she bade Alphonse to stay. When they were alone with only Maria's scribes and servants, she commanded one of the scribes to draw up a deed for this precious forty hectares, about one hundred acres, and to gift this land to Alphonse Herrera and his progeny for as long as the sun and the moon were in the skies.

It was a month later that Alphonse stood gazing at the wonderful gift his loving queen had bestowed upon him. Having used some of the gold coin to purchase thirty cuttings of Tempranillo red grape and another thirty of Palomino white, "*Por favor,*" he addressed the white puffy clouds above him, "What do I do now?"

Now six hundred years later, Rene Mendoza cast an experienced watch over the vast vineyard. His practiced eyes swept from the hillside down to the lake. He so badly wished for a glimpse of the raccoons that had nightly raided his holdings and fed sumptuously on his beautiful Palomino grapes.

He held the new Winchester model 1866 confidently. This fine rifle had been shipped to him from a place called Connecticut in America. Only the wealthy could afford such a fine imported arm, but Mendoza was wealthy indeed. His fine vineyard was one of his nation's best, and his Spanish wines were famous around the globe.

He moved his studied gaze to the foot of the hill where the three-story brick structure that was the winery stood. His overseer, Hector, and his crew of ten were loading fruit into the horse drawn elevator that would move the harvest to the third floor of the massive brick and mortar structure.

Using the force of gravity, the fruit would move from the highest point in the building to the lowest, being exposed to one process or another as it traveled downward. Three months later, it would be wine. Some for immediate sale, and some to be stored for aging, and to become the headliner of the Mendoza wines collection.

The massive arbor had stood here for many generations of Mendozas. No one knew, or could remember, how it had come to be in the first place. The passing of time and the countless harvests of grape had erased any recollection of the vineyard's origin.

As a devout Christian, he first recounted his blessings before asking God's help with his troubles. Here was his fortune—a splendid house, faithful wife, three strong sons, and a beautiful daughter. There was a barn with fine horses, more than fifty employees, and more gold and silver coin than he could count in the depository in the village of Acadia. It was the third son. It was Antoine who was Rene Mendoza's only problem in life.

"Juanita," he spoke to the stout lady who was his wife. "We must talk of Antoine. I fear we must send him away."

She blanched at the suggestion. "I know what he is, Rene, but even knowing, my heart would break were he not here."

Rene held up his hand. "He is ruining the reputation of our family. His own brothers have shunned him, and what chance will Esmerelda have for a good marriage with what is happening. No! We will speak no more of this. I will give him money. He will live well. I will send him to America. He can open a warehouse and we will sell our grapes in America. He is *maricón*. He cannot stay."

"*Maricón*? Are you sure, Rene? Is it true our son has taken another man for a lover? Are we sure?"

Rene shook his head sadly. "All of Acadia knows this. I must send him away—for all of us—for our family."

Juanita Mendoza dabbed at her eyes with a small perfumed handkerchief. "But where will he go? America is a big place—dangerous, too."

"I am told there are many Frenchmen in the place that is New Orleans. The French are likely to be more forgiving of our son's preferences. I will give him money, and we will send him to New Orleans"

"Dear Rene," his wife besought, "what about my brother Christof? Have you thought of him? He would surely be willing to help our son and his nephew. He is godfather to Antoine. If Antoine went to be with him, he would not be alone in such a place as America."

"He cannot go to Christof, Juanita. Christof lives in a place called Kansas. I think people in Kansas do not drink wine—no, he must go to New Orleans. I will give him money—he will do well. This I will do today! This very day!"

Chapter Five

New Orleans, 1872

Once Amber had made up her mind to seek protection from the prizefighter, Antoine Acadia, she wasted not a moment. It was still early afternoon as she stood and gaped at the disheveled bistro that was Tracy's. It was the kind of establishment that might easily have a new sign within a week, or even disappear forever.

Dirty windows, unswept stoop, and the foul odor of spilled and soured warm beer assaulted her senses as she tried to muster the fortitude to enter this little den of foul odors, and its indiscriminate feeling of danger.

Summer heat added to the humidity of the darkened room. A few early drinkers were seated about, some in various stages of drunkenness. *Bar flies*, she thought, *drunks with no place to go. Queer folk. Only they are welcome here.*

"I don't know what you're lookin' for, sweetheart, but I think you're in the wrong place. It may be good honey, but this is not your market." It was the barman who rallied enough energy to address her.

44

"I'd like to see Mister Acadia—Antoine Acadia," Amber called out in a voice that sounded strange even to herself.

"I'm here, little miss," a deep voice resounded from the darkest corner of the room.

"Aw, looky here," the barman went on. "Tony went and got hisself a little pony. Here's Tony's pony, boys—a sweet little puta…"

"Enough, Pasquale!" The voice from the corner was a rough and a ready indictment.

"You always just take things too serious, Tony— too seriously. It's why you have no amigos around here—no compadres." The barman returned to his glass polishing.

Antoine Acadia stood from his table, secured within the shadowy corner of Tracy's Bistro's barroom. As he emerged from the shadows into the pale light of the barroom, Amber once again recalled how taken she had been at his boxing match with his physical attractiveness.

Tall, muscular and roguishly handsome, she felt a slight shiver as he neared her. "Sit here," he told her, as he pulled a chair from a nearby table and offered it to her. He arranged another seat across from her for himself.

"Two coffees, Pasquale," he called. "Very hot. Very sweet. Tell me senorita, why have you come? What would you wish from me?"

He is the most goodest-lookin' man I've ever seen, she thought. She was silent until the barman brought the coffee. "I'm sore in need've protection," she began. "I need help from someone strong, tough—someone who ain't afraid." Amber took a long time to tell Antoine of her troubles with the Daniel Ricardo affair.

She described the wedding proposal and how she knew it was a ploy for Ricardo to own her completely. Not for love, but for her earnings as a street walker.

"He was just wantin' me for a pony," she said. "I just found out he has other ponies, I think. I'm not for really sure, but I thinks so." She explained to him how she longed to leave the street, but she had to earn money and save it in order for that to ever happen.

"And when you have enough money to leave the street," he asked, "what will you do then?"

"I will rent myself a house, I will," she said. "When I have a house, I will become a madam. I will leave this harbor area and find me a house in Picayune or Trocadero area. I will employ three— no, four young ladies. I will make them and myself rich, and together we will leave the street forever.

"Then I will be a lady. I will attend church. I'm gonna learn to play the piano. I'm gonna feed the street urchins. I'm gonna do all these things. I promise that I will."

"And all these fine things will happen when I kill this Daniel Ricardo for you?"

"Oh, not kill!" Amber was horrified. "Not killed, just scared away. Maybe beat him up—not kill though."

"Sweet Amber, you do not know how things work do you?" His voice was as attractive as was the rest of him. He spoke perfect English with just enough of a slight accent to identify his Spanish heritage.

"If I were to beat this Daniel, in a day or two his workers would then beat me. I would then get my friends, and we would beat them, and on and on it would go. If I were to kill this Daniel, it would end, and you could rent your house, find your three, no, four girls and make your fortune."

"But," Amber challenged, "if you killed him, wouldn't his workers then kill you?"

"Not at all. If he was dead, there would be no one to pay them. Without pay, they would do nothing."

"I could never do that," Amber said. "I only wanted to scare him away. I couldn't see him dead."

"And one more thing, Senorita Amber. Were you planning to pay me for this service...and how much?"

"I have saved sixty-three dollars, and that was what I would offer you. That was for beatin' him though. I understand that would not be enough to cause you to do murder."

"This sixty-three dollars, these are dollars you have saved to rent the house?"

"No. That is what I call my first money. The house savings is my second money, and I would never touch that."

Antoine took a pause for a moment. "And how much do you have in this second money?"

"I ain't tell'n' you," she replied. "Not how much, nor where it is. I will tell you this. I don't keep it at my rooms. It is well hidden."

"I see. That is wise. I am thinking there may be another way. Suppose you and I go together and talk to this Daniel. Perhaps we could get him to listen to reason."

The next day, Amber and Antoine began their search for Daniel Ricardo. Amber liked the idea of trying to reason with Daniel. Especially as she was in the presence of this man who was obviously a great deal more physically powerful than Daniel.

It was on the third day of their search they happened by a bench in one of the small parks that provided a bit of green space in an otherwise grey and cobble-colored city.

"Sit here by me," Antoine asked her. Already tired from the three-day search, Amber quite happily obliged. "I feel we must talk, Amber. Our plan is not working."

"You think not?" she asked.

"Not at all." he replied.

"But I feel we'll spot him any day…anytime now."

Antoine stood up beside her. She sensed he had something serious to say. "You haven't been watching closely enough, Amber. He's already found us. I've seen him and his two companions twice already this morning."

"Oh! Where?" she cried.

"Peering at us from the doorways and that alley on Megs Way. I'm afraid that means we must change our plan. He's no longer afraid of us—of me. He probably has guns, Amber. He's not hiding from us, he's out to kill us now, or at least, kill you."

Shaken, Amber was visibly upset. "I never meant for it to go this far," she said. "I only hoped we could scare him—frighten him away."

"Listen to me carefully, Amber. I will deal with Ricardo. You go to your home and pack a bag of the things you will need. We must leave the city—at least for a while. Bring your money, Amber. I'm not sure when we'll be able to return."

"I won't bring my money!" she cried. "You only want to steal it from me."

"Bring everything you must have, Amber. When I deal with Ricardo, we will not be able to stay here longer. You must trust me with this. I will not deceive you."

"But how can I trust you? I barely know you. Who are you that you would commit murder for me? Run away from your home for me?"

"Amber, this is not my home. I have already run from my home. You must trust me because I have become your friend. You have become my ward. I will always protect you. It is a code my family has lived by for centuries. You need not understand it— at least not right now. Honestly, I think there may come a time that you may do something for me that I want, that I need very badly. Go and gather your things. Meet me here by this bench. Meet me here at sundown today. We will take a train from this place. I will have the tickets. If I am to do what I think I must, we must leave here tonight."

"But Antoine," she whimpered, "even if I decide to trust you, where can we go? Will we ever be safe?"

"I have an uncle who loves me. He is very rich, and he will love you, too. Tonight, we leave—we will ride a train. We go to Kansas."

Chapter Six

Saint Anne's Parish

"Homer! Homer!" she pleaded. Mavis Chastain was diligently trying to awaken her sleeping husband. The slumbering constable groaned as he tried vainly to awaken himself.

"What is it, Mavis? What'sa matter?"

"It's the door, Homer! Someone's pounding on the door! For Christ sakes. Can't you hear all that commotion?" The constable of Saint Anne's Bayou Parish was now sleepily aware of a loud and persistent pounding at the front door.

"Go, Mavis!" he retorted. "For Christ sake, go see who that is beatin' the damn door down! I'm a havin' a helluva time wakin' up. Go see to it. See who is that."

"Go your own self, damn it. I'm naked. I don't know how the hell you can sleep in all this heat anyway. Get the door! Whoever's out there's wakening the whole damn Basin Street neighborhood."

The sleepy constable knew it was futile to argue with his wife of ten years. On the rare occasion when Mavis used hard language mixed with her native Creole, her resolve was carved in stone. He stirred himself and looked at her pouting face. In the dusky glow of dawn's first light piercing the half-shaded window, she was even more beautiful to him than ever.

A statuesque Creole beauty he had married in a bayou torch light ceremony a decade ago, she nevertheless excited him to this day. Realizing arguing with her this day was futile, he surrendered and groggily made his way to his front door.

Careful as to who might be the other side of the door, he cracked it slightly and peered out. The sun was barely starting to appear in the east. Still nearly dark, it was, however, just light enough for Homer to recognize his deputy, Julio Esparza.

"What the hell do you want, Julie?" the sleepy Homer barked. "What're you doin' here afore daylight?"

"D-de-dead man," Julio stammered, "dead body down on dock six! Couple o' Creole boys come around the office 'bout half hour ago. Found this here dead fellow, they did—down on six—Oyster dock—I come right here for you."

"You lock up them two—them Creoles?"

"Lock 'em up?" The deputy looked puzzled.

"Yeah—they probably what made him dead."

"No, didn't think that—shoulda', I guess. No. They went back to the dock. I tell them go and stay by the dead man till Constable Homer come. They went right away. They there, I 'spect."

"I hope you're right, Julie. Go on down there and I'll be along soon's I can get some clothes on—no wait! Better go get Doc Grimes first. He gonna want to see this body. In this heat he ain't gonna have long to do whatever he needs to do. Go on now, I be there soon's I can." Homer returned now to the bedroom and began to search about in the half-light for his clothing.

"Heard that," Mavis said. "Got a dead man on the docks. What is that? Four this month?"

"Three, I think—seems every summer, when it really gets hot, folks just cain't hardly control they selves. Get to fightin'. Somebody dead afore you know it." He moved about searching for his shirt in the morning semidarkness. As he neared his wife, he became aware she was nude. He could not resist reaching out and playfully seizing a generous handful of one of her butt cheeks.

"Get the hell away from me, Homer. It's too damn hot for any of that."

"Man needs a little lovin' now and then, Mavis," he whined.

"Come see me in October, Homer. Maybe Christmas," she chided. "Now get out of here and go play with your dead body."

It was nearly ten by the time Homer hitched his buggy and drove his flighty mare the three miles to the dock area. August heat was well in force by now. The sun was hot and the air thin, and waves of glassy heat shimmered the view of the watery delta.

Although Constable Chastain was proud of his blue uniform, it was oppressive to him now. Just as Homer Chastain made it to dock six, Doctor Grimes was about to stretch a cover over the limp form lying in the broiling, midmorning Louisiana sun. Still, he took a moment to gaze at his surroundings. Here he could see the muddy waters of the great Mississippi pour into the pristine seawaters that made up the Gulf of Mexico. Its majesty never failed to astound him.

"Hold it Doc," Homer called. "Let me have a peep."

Doctor Grimes, a florid-faced, overweight man in his late sixties, replied, "Right on, Homer. Come have a see."

The experienced constable, in his twelfth year as a New Orleans lawman, had indeed looked upon a great number of corpses during his tenure. This one, though, was especially disturbing. It was obviously the body of a young man in the prime of his life, but Homer Chastain had never encountered a body so brutally beaten.

"This is not somebody killed in a fist fight that got out of control," the Doctor allowed. "This here was an intentional killing. A murder! Probably somebody pretty mad about something. Not a robbery either. He's got quite a bit of money in his folder...a good watch, too. Your man, the deputy, says couple of Creole boys claim they found him dead. I reckon that's the truth—else they'd taken that money—that good watch for sure."

"Had much dealin's with the Creole folks hereabout, have you, Doc?" Homer asked.

"Naw, fetch 'em a couple of whelps. Cleaned-up two or three after some hellacious knife fightin's."

"I been dealin' with 'em a long time now—married one, you know? Tell you somethin' I know 'bout French Creole. You question one of these local Creole boys about his honor, and he'll kill you sure as hell. Same was you to say somethin' harsh about his wife or daughter, you'd like be dead afore you hit the ground. When it comes to stealin' though—robbin', or foot paddin', or the like—been my experience they ain't much for that. They's mostly Catholics, you know, and likely the best Catholics you'd be able to find. If this here dead fella offended their honor, they might well have done for him. They wouldn't do that for no watch, I think. No—this was somebody really bent on a killing. It may

55

have been them Creoles though. Depends on what was between them and him."

Doctor Grimes interjected, "Got a question for you though, Homer. Why, if it was them, would they show up at your place reporting him dead?"

"It's the old story about the drunken fox."

"How's that?"

"This here fox shows up at the vintner's wine store. He's so drunk, he can't hardly walk at all. Claims he saw the goat drinkin' up all the wine stored in the barn."

"Ah, I see what you mean, Homer. Here's somethin' else though. Look here at this lesion on the side of the head. Ever see anything like that afore?"

The wound pointed out by the Parish coroner was unlike any injury Homer had encountered previously. A large dent in the side of the head near the crown. The skull had seemed to just give way from some horrendous blow, leaving a bowl-shaped depression.

"Caved his head right in, huh? Just busted right through the skull. No, I never seen anything like that. Any weapon laying around that could have caused it? Did you find anything?"

"Look careful, Homer. Does that look like what a fist could do...I mean, could do if someone could hit hard enough?"

"You mean a punch? I don't think that's likely. I don't think anyone could do that with just his fist. Though I see what you mean. It looks like a fist. I just don't think that could be—though maybe..."

"Ever hear tell of a man named John L. Sullivan?"

"What? The fighter?"

"It's been said he's probably goin' to be the champeen boxer of the whole world someday. Some say he can kill a horse with a right-hand punch. Claims he did it at a carnival up in Boston."

Homer only thought for a moment. "Well, tell you right now, Doc. Was I to see a man hit a horse like that, I'd bury his ass in one of my special cells, and nobody would never see him no more."

"You got special cells, have you, Homer?"

"Got some old prison holes Andy Jackson built back in 1815. Put some redcoat colonels away in there, I hear. They was supposed to be let out after the war, but somehow they's just forgot about. Found 'em 'bout twenty years later, I hear. May not be true, but what is true is them holes are pretty bad. Pretty awful, they are. Lots of rats. Underground too—no sunshine. Haven't ever used 'em afore. Man beat a horse to death, and I might."

Doctor Grimes fished in his vest for a cigar. "Anyway, somebody sure finished this here old boy for good. I wonder if we'll be able to find out who he is?"

"Oh hell, Doc, I ain't for sure what happened to him, but I know who he is."

"You do?"

"Name's Ricardo—somethin' like that. I've arrested him four or five times. Calls himself a whoremaster. Shit. Just a street corner pimp is all he was. Rolled a few drunks, too. Robbed some workin' girls of a few bucks. Not sure what he did to end up like this, but I'd say he got the wrong guy mad at him. Else the sky just fell in on him. Course in this summer warmth, almost anybody can lose control. This heat's just maddenin'."

That same morning, less than two miles away, Abner Willet was experiencing one of his most perplexing days. Not only was the bank's interior approaching oven temperature, he was beginning to have self-doubts as to his ability as a banker.

"It's just not reasonable," he said nearly aloud to himself. "A depositor like that, and I don't even know he's a customer?" He reached for his humidor at the edge of the desk, then reconsidered. "Too hot to smoke," he muttered. "Too damn hot."

Twenty-two years ago, Abner had accepted the job as president of the Coleman American Bank and Trust Company. It was not a position he had applied for, but rather one he had been assigned to by his wife's father, Alfred W. Coleman the Third. It was a job with club privileges and access to the society realm of New Orleans so important to Abner's wife, Julianna.

In spite of the tedium of perusing day to day columns of figures and the sheer boredom sitting at his desk day to day awaiting something to happen, he had at last settled into his presidency. He had actually begun to enjoy those about him treating him with a type of respect and reverence normally reserved for royalty. But today, he had encountered an incident that was upsetting his normally mundane existence.

"Chester!" he called out to his head cashier. "Chester, I need you. Come here. Quickly—Chester, come."

Weak eyed and mopping his sweating bald pate with a large bandana, the myopic Chester Worth made his way into the authoritative grandeur of the presidential office.

"Yes sir. What can I do for you?"

"I want to know, did you see that man that just left my office—that big fellow?"

"Why yes, I surely did, Mister Willet, sir. He would be hard to miss."

"Ever seen him before? Here in the bank?"

The cashier answered instantly, "No sir. Not here in the bank. But I've seen him. I know who he is. One of those boxers who brawl down in the dock area on Saturday. You know. Where the gamblers are. Seen him there, lots o' times."

"Fighter? He's a fighter?"

"True as daylight, he is. Seen him just last week."

"You attend those spectacles, Chester?" The president seemed dismayed.

"Oh no sir," Chester lied. "Oh, I just heard that Marvin Bass—you know—our window number three. I heard he was there, and I knew you'd not approve. I just went there to fetch him. I did."

"Bass? Marvin Bass? Anyway—well, here's the thing—that fellow just came in and had me transfer his entire balance to some bank way the hell off in Kansas somewhere. How come we've had his money more than two years and I've never seen him even once?"

"Well," Chester began, "I'd suppose a man like himself would hardly have enough money to call your attention to it. Just a street brawler and all."

"Would you think I'd pay attention to ninety thousand dollars?"

"What's that, sir?" The cashier was incredulous.

"Ninety thousand! That's what I said. Do you realize that man—that fighter, was one of the chief depositors we had, and we've never even said 'hello' to him? And then I wonder, where the hell would a street fighter get that kind of revenue? Why would he leave it here two years, with not one single transaction in all that time? Not one deposit...not one withdrawal! Then, just suddenly walks in and withdraws it all? Transfers it to Kansas? Kansas, for God's sake. There's still wild Indians in Kansas! I tell you, Chester, this whole thing just smells to me."

"I can see why, sir. It just smells. Good thing your astute enough to catch it. Most of us here at the bank would've missed it for sure. But you, sir. You caught it right away."

"Tell you what, Chester. You take a walk over to Constable Chastain's office. Tell him I'd like to see him. This bank has never had a withdrawal that large. Something here needs looking into."

"Yes sir. It surely needs looking into. Should I go after close?"

"No—go now. Go right now," Abner insisted.

"Yes sir! Right now! On my way."

"On your way out, tell Marvin Bass at window three I want to see him."

–oOo–

The moment Antoine caught up with Amber at the Louisiana, Arkansas, Kansas City Southern train terminal on South Rampart Street, she wanted to know, "What about Daniel?" Her anxiety was apparent. "Is he—is he dead? Did you…?"

"No, not dead. He's just fine. More's the pity."

"Could you not find him?" Amber was trembling now.

"Oh, I found him. He's well enough to be involved in more mischief, you can be assured. Frankly, I was well prepared to do what needed to be done, but all of a sudden, it didn't need to be done any more. I don't think you're on his mind anymore, Amber. At least as much as you were. Got himself a pretty little Creole pony now. Pretty little thing. Be hard to think of old Amber with this little trick around."

"Tell me what…what happened." Amber was impatient now.

"Nothing, nothing at all. I caught up with him down by the docks. Told him to leave you alone—and me. He said to tell you to go to hell! Not interested in you at all—wishes he had never asked you to marry him—took his little pony by the hand, thumbed his nose at me, and walked away."

"Oh, Antoine, I'm so glad you didn't have to do what we planned. So glad."

"Well, I guess I am, too, Amber, now that it's over. Was a time I was actually looking forward to putting that strutting rooster in his place. Just lucky he found this pretty little girl—his style, too. I'd say she's 'bout fourteen. Fifteen maybe. Anyway, we're done with Daniel Ricardo—you and me—end of it all. No more trouble from him—not ever."

"But if it's settled, are we still leaving? Why?"

"Amber, you should understand, Daniel Ricardo hates you. Remember how he stalked you? Had I not been there, he would have killed you for sure. As soon as his fascination fades with this new little girl, he's going to be on your trail again. You'll never be safe on the street again. Better I should have killed him, but there was the girl. Also, I saw two young men near the area—shrimpers maybe. I could not take him down with them around. The way it's worked out—just better that we go. Who knows what's in store for us? A better life, I think. My Uncle and Aunt will welcome us—of this I'm sure. I am afraid it's all that I am sure of though," he added.

Amber stared out of the train window at the ebony dark as the Texas Flyer made her way across the Louisiana border, and into the Arkansas night. She sat in a seat directly across from the sleeping Antoine Acadia, and again she found herself assessing his uncommonly handsome visage.

She had never been on a train before and had indeed never even considered that she someday might be. This whole experience was new to her and more than a little frightening. At seventeen years old, it was true she had some doubtful moments due to her profession. They, frightening as they may have been, were less unsettling than the situation she now found herself encountering.

She still wondered if she could trust Antoine. And, of course, over and over she asked herself, *What's happening? Where am I going? What's going to happen to me when I get to Kansas?*

–oOo–

When secretary Laverne Emery announced the arrival of Constable Chastain, Abner Willet was only a few moments from exploding with rage.

"Damn it, Homer, you sure took your sweet time getting your ass over here."

"Easy Abner—take it easy. Hot day like this you're like to keel over. I'm here. What the hell do you want?" Banker Willet mopped his damp brow with a nicely stitched silken handkerchief.

"I have been robbed! I mean I don't know whether I been robbed or not. *Might* have been robbed, I mean."

"Just hold on, Abner. Take it easy for a minute or two and tell me what's goin' on here. Robbed? Who robbed you? How?"

"This here fighting fellow, boxer man—comes in and takes out ninety thousand dollars, he does! Just up and withdraws ninety thousand dollars. Just like that. Takes ninety thousand dollars and just walks right out of here as proud as you please."

"Hang on, Abner." Homer was struggling to understand. "Did I catch it you said this here boxer feller withdrew some money? Don't that mean the money was his? And he just took it out of the bank?"

"Damn right. Took it right out. Ninety thousand dollars. That's more'n a third of all the money in this fuckin' bank. Ninety thousand—just like that!"

"A third, huh?" Homer Chastain was mentally calculating. "Your sign outside says this here bank's got five million on deposit."

"Ain't my sign—that's my father-in-law's sign. Put that up there before my time here, he did. Just in case you ain't heard, we had ourselves a little scrap called the Civil War since then. By the way, we lost. What little was left carpetbaggers been hauling it off since sixty-five. Five million! There ain't five million in the whole damn state of Louisiana since the war.

"I figure New Orleans lost fifty million in slaves alone. Cotton—gone. Blooded horses—all stolen. Plantations—just in ruins." Abner was growing despondent. Homer seated himself in a mahogany Queen Anne chair directly across from the front of Abner's desk.

"Do you know why you lose money at our Wednesday night game every single week, Abner? Do you know?"

"What the hell are you talking about? What's that got to do with the bank's money?" Abner wanted to know. "I certainly do not lose money every Wednesday. That's total bullshit!"

"Every single Wednesday, Abner, we get fifty or sixty bucks of your wife's butter and egg money. Fifty-two Wednesdays every year, me and Howie, Slim and the Turk can count on you leaving us our lunch money for the week. Do you know what makes that happen, Abner? It's just like right now. You get so damned excited. Every time you get a good hand you light up grinnin' like a possum eatin' shit. We know that, so we fold. You win a pot of a few quarters. When the pot's pretty good, though, we can always raise you till you panic—make you quit. That's what you're doing right now—getting too excited. What man? What happened?"

"Antoine Acadia, his name is. Big guy. Scary as hell. I hear he's one of them bare knuckle fighters down to the wharf. Took out all his money. Most folks just draw some when they need it. Took it all and just walked out. I checked back. He put that money in here more'n three years ago—never comes back till this morning. Not even once. I'm thinkin' something's really wrong here, and then you don't show up till afternoon. What the hell was you doin' all morning anyhow?" Homer rose from his chair and, by hitching his belt, made it apparent he was leaving.

"Matter of fact I was at the wharf myself this morning. All morning. Dead man. All beat to hell."

"See! See!" Abner sprang from his chair. "Could be this here Acadia fellow killed your dead man—I mean killed your man—made him dead. Come got his money. Gettin' out of here with his money. Probably long gone by now. You could've moved your ass a little faster, maybe could have got him. Questioned him anyhow."

"That's pretty far-fetched, Abner. I will go down to the train depot, though, and ask if any unusuals caught any trains. Is old man Winslow still ticket master down there, do you think? Do you reckon he's still there?"

"Course he's still there! Where the hell else would an old fart like Pap Winslow be? Dead maybe? Not dead? Bet your ass he's there. Can you move your ass a little? Find out where's my money? Er—bank's money?"

"Do the best I can, Abner. Promise you that—do the best I can. If I don't see you sooner, I'll see you at the card club Wednesday night."

"Your ass!"

Chapter Seven

Nineteen years earlier, San Caption, Spain

The sea was a wonderment to Christof Romero. Having lived the entirety of his twenty-three years within the town of Acadia and its nearby environs, he had never before beheld such open space, and was never so intoxicated by the excess of sounds and smells.

As he walked along the dock area, he diligently searched for a ship among the half dozen anchorages with the name of *Alexandria*. It was at the very end of the plank boardwalk that he encountered his prize. Three masts above a plank vessel she turned out to be. *The Alexandria* was built somewhat along the lines of a sloop, yet broader with a stouter appearance. The sealed gun ports along her topside revealed that at some point in her life she had been a ship of war. Now converted to a more mundane hauler of people and freight, she lived a more peaceful span.

Weather had seasoned her planking to a greyish tan. But at her rear, from a slanted pole, she sported an American flag of the red, white, and blue. The flag was a furl of red and white stripes with a quarter field of blue scattered with white stars. A breeze from the west fluttered the flag just enough so that Christof was unable to count her stars, but he knew well enough there were thirty-one. He had read extensively and studied the American story greatly since the day, more than two years ago, he had determined this new land across the Atlantic was to be his new home. Actually, America was near two hundred fifty or so years old since her first settlers had braved the Atlantic. It was a mere babe, though, when compared to the rolling centuries of historic Europe and Spain

It was true that his life in Acadia was a remarkably good one. His sister marrying into the Mendoza family had assured him a lucrative position in one of the world's most recognized vineyards and wineries. Nonetheless, these were the properties of his brother-in-law. He so longed for something of his very own, and something built by him for his future offspring—something entirely belonging to himself and God.

The acquisition of land in Spain, Portugal or anywhere in Europe was literally impossible. Generations and centuries upon centuries of traditional ownership had put the acquiring of land beyond the reach of all but the wealthiest or titled aristocracy.

Those who were lenders would loan worthy men funds for the purchase of a cow, perhaps, or maybe a draft horse to command a plow. To approach one of these and ask for finances to purchase real property, though, was simply a waste of time.

In America, though, the one ingredient vital for success could be had. Land could be owned by anyone with courage enough to risk all on one throw of pitch and toss. He knew, within his heart, he was that man.

It was at the morning hour of nine as prearranged, he met with Captain Michael O'Fallon, master of the vessel *Alexandria.*

"You'd sail with me to California, would ye? You'll be safe enough. The *Alexandria* has made that voyage four times now. It's the test of a good vessel and seamanship as well. Still, this is not a voyage to be taken lightly. It's the roughest, wildest sea spree of all." Michael O'Fallon was a stoutly built man with a well-trimmed, reddish beard. Clothed in a sailor's blue coat and peaked captain's cap with gold braid across its bill, he looked as seaworthy as the *Alexandria* herself. Christof's first impression of him was one of an honest, open man. He was confident and much experienced.

"With a name as O'Fallon, I'd expect you're of Irish lineage."

"As sure as a shamrock, I am." A slight brogue was detected.

"I've heard the tales of rough seas about the Cape of Horn," Christof said. "Are they as great a danger as we are told?"

"First off, you need to understand," Captain O'Fallon went on. "For more'n a hundred years, no man sailed thereabouts except explorer types and a few men of science. Men such as you, who wanted to get to California, sailed to Boston or South Carolina—Georgia maybe. Then traveled overland. Nine, ten months or a year maybe. Sail from Spain around the Horn and you're in Frisco six or seven weeks. Came 1849—the rush has been on ever since. They's a chandler shop in Frisco keeps a tally. Just short of seven thousand souls in the past two years braved the Horn. Now, here you are one more, and thirty like you, on this here voyage. Thirty-one more to seek California gold."

"Gold? Did you think I was a gold hunter?"

"What else is there? No one heads to California any more on a chancy voyage like this if not for riches. All I've seen since forty-nine and the Sutter's mill nuggets were found is those lookin' for the yellow trace."

"Not gold—it's grapes—grapes I want. Grapes brought to the Pacific coast by Spanish Grandees and Isabella's knights back in the fifteen-hundreds.

Grapes with more than two hundred years of successful tradition. Not gold. Palomino, Mataro and Tempranillo. These are the treasures I seek." The captain's eyes widened.

"By Gar! Grapes, is it? I'm thinkin' a grape is a grape. Not so I see. It's a vintner that you are, and that's plain enough for the likes of me. I've seen naught but gold seekers for so long, I've forgotten there are other things that are good in California."

"I'm told there exists vineyards about California that are more than two hundred years old. I'm bound eventually for a place named Kansas, and I mean to transport all the cuttings from vineyards like that I'm able to carry."

"By the thunder! It's so good to meet a man like yourself." O'Fallon was nearly jubilant. "Honest work you want. You're seeking a credible life and not a bonanza. We'll sail the Horn together, and I'll set you ashore in Frisco, and you can seek out your grapes! It's fine work you're about. There's nothing so entertaining as a glass o' good grape."

"The fruit I search for was never meant for entertainment. To these men who tended the vineyards so long ago, the wine they created was the holy blood of Jesus, the Christ, our Lord. I am told of hundreds of missions built by these early Spaniards. Isabella had sent these great evangelists to tell the story of the love of the Christ to the savage of the land. The celebration of communion requires wine. It must be perfect wine if it is to replace the blood of our savior. I look forward to the day that I might craft a wine of such wonderful character."

"Are you a priest then? A priest in the garb of a vagabond traveler?"

"Not a priest...just a man. A knight, if you will. A knight on a mission. I would help others to recall the last supper of our Lord and my brother, the Son of God. As I am, too, a son of God. But enough on that. Captain O'Fallon, could you just be good enough to tell me a bit of what I should expect? Just how fearful is this voyage—this place where the Atlantic and Pacific meet?"

"They do not meet. They collide! Something fearful happens when these two great ocean seas converge upon each other that no one can explain rightly. We'll sail betwixt the tip of South America and the upper edge of Antarctica. Home of the South Pole. High winds filled with sleet that can shred a sail. Fifty-foot swells and waves of sixty feet can occur and do in the blink of an eye. If you fly too much canvas, you'll drive your bow to the bottom of those swells. Too little, and you'll yield control to the winds and the sea. With nearly two hundred miles, you'll hope you can beat the squalls."

"Isn't there any other way?" Christof wanted to know. "Some way safer?"

"They's two more ways to go. I'm not sure about safer. Eighty miles north of the Horn lay the straits of Magellan. You can navigate through those and miss some of the high winds. Problem is, the straits ain't very straight. They weave and meander through a great shoal of high rocky banks and cliffs. These passage walls are sometimes less than a mile apart and thirty miles long. Then comes the tradeoff—you'll avoid some of the Antarctic wind and trade it for the thickest fog banks you can imagine. Try to think about sailing through those rocky cliffs when you can't see to count your fingers. The other way is the Isthmus of Panama. You can put into that narrow neck of Panama and walk west for forty miles, and another ship will meet you on the Pacific side to bear you north to Frisco."

"Can't you ride a coach or wagon?" Christof wanted to know.

"It's a boggy swamp," was the answer. "No wagon, mud, heat, flies, poison serpents—mosquitos big enough to stand flat-footed and violate a turkey. Add to this a cadre of bandits determined to see that you never reach the Pacific. No, if you go with me lad, you'll sail the Horn."

"I guess that's it then. Could I serve some on the crew? To pay some of my passage. I've never sailed before, but I can follow orders."

"I've got six able men. We always need galley help though. Think you could help ship's cook keep us alive?"

"Give my word I'll try, sir. Try my best."

"Well, there she is then. Six men and you make seven. Seven men and my daughter."

"Daughter? You sail with your daughter aboard?"

"You'll see her soon enough. She dresses like the men, but you'll know her right off. She'll be the one that's the boldest—the one who jumps to the task and never shirks. She'll be the one whose works are the best of all. Charlotte O'Fallon is the best sea dog aboard the *Alexandria.*"

Chapter Eight

Oceola, Kansas 1872

Although Amber and Antoine had been together for several days, there were so many things that they had not spoken of.

"How, Amber," Antoine wanted to know, "have you come to be in the business you are in? It seems so unlikely for you—so young—so pretty. I imagine you could do many things."

"Oh my," Amber allowed. "No one has ever asked me that before. Ha! Antoine, you are like all men—that's the one question every man I've ever met thought they had to know the answer to." Amber took a long and very deep breath as she considered her answer. "Some of us have no choices, Antoine. We take what we are given and try to live with it—just do the best we can."

"I think you could do other things—find some work—a job, maybe."

"A job? Oh, I had a job." Amber resigned herself to telling the story she had recounted to herself so many times. Antoine, though, would be the first person, either man or woman, to hear it.

"Momma died when I was twelve," she started. "Papa and me—we lived in a boarding house. Miss Macomber's boarding house. Papa worked—worked every day—shrimper. Every day at sundown, I'd come to the docks to meet him. We'd sometimes go home to supper or sometimes go the Green Frog and eat red fish together." Amber paused here as she recalled a favorite memory.

"Papa and I were doin' good. Evenings, he'd sit at a big, old chair in our room and he'd tell me all about his day. Sometimes he'd drink whiskey. Not all the time, but sometimes. When he did, he'd cry about Momma. One night, I went to bed and left Papa sitting in that chair. He cried a little that night—drunker than usual I'd guess. Anyhow, next morning he was gone, just gone. Never came back. I waited and waited—just gone—never saw him again—ever." She stared out the train window at the darkness.

"What did you do then?" Antoine was deeply moved by this story of sadness.

"Miss Macomber—she let me stay awhile, but I had only a few dollars Papa left behind, and when that was gone, well, she said she needed to have the room, and I should go to Saint Agnes's and maybe the nuns could help me find Papa. I was at Saint Agnes's a long time—with a lot of other girls—a long time. Then one day, a man came and Sister

Carmel said I should go with him—me and two others—Yvonne and Claudia."

"He took you where?" Antoine wanted to know. "Who was this man?"

"We went to this big place called a dormitory. Lots of other girls there. I found out later it was a prison. A big jail."

"Jail? Prison?" Antoine was dumbfounded.

"Yes, but I was not a prisoner. Some of the girls were chained at night. Yvonne and Claudia and I, though, were free. Free—except for the job I told you about. I went to this huge factory where we sewed work clothes—you know—pants and shirts and so on. I loved the sewing—I was so good at it after a while—I thought I could just sew things forever, but the days were long—long, hard—I worked ten hours each day for six days a week. I was given seven dollars and fifty cents every Saturday night. Except this man they called the steward took a dollar each week from me to be sure I would be allowed to work the next week. I had to pay for the room at the dormitory and the two meals I had there daily. Not much to eat—thin soup—sometimes wheat or corn porridge, chickory coffee. Anyhow, that was the job—you asked if I could get work? That was the job."

"I feel so sorry," Antoine allowed. "So, sorry."

"Claudia ran away first—then Yvonne. They found some rooms near the docks and started seeing men for money. Then they came for me and when I learned I could earn seven or eight dollars each night, well I walked away from my sewing—walked away, and here I am."

"Did the sisters at Saint Agnes ever talk to you about sin? About God?" Antoine asked.

"Oh, good gracious yes. I love Jesus gooder than anything. When I can—when I'm rich enough I'm gonna be a Christian."

"I didn't know one must be rich in order to be a Christian."

"Well, you certainly do. You got to have some money to be anything—anything at all. You cain't be no Christian nor nothin' else if you're poor's Job's turkey. Once I get me some money, I'm goin' to be a devout."

"When might that be?" Antoine wanted to know.

"Well, you gotta be set in life before you can be a Christian—I mean, a good Christian. You gotta have somethin' to put in the church plate on Sunday. You cain't be a worryin' whether you gonna have enough to eat and still think about heaven. Bein' hungry *is* hell, you know? Have you ever been hungry, Antoine? Cold? Alone and hungry? Ever take bread out of someone's garbage? Eat food someone made up for their dog?"

"No," Antoine thoughtfully answered.

"Me neither," Amber replied. "But was I to leave the street—stop doin' what I'm doin'—it wouldn't take long for me to be right there. Lots of other girls I know are. I just ain't rich enough yet to love Jesus like I need to. When I get the house and when things are better for me—well, then—well, then we gonna see."

"Are you ever scared.? Do the men ever frighten you?"

"At first I hated being undressed, but then I saw how the men enjoyed it—how they looked at me. It felt good after a while. Sometimes I'm scared, but I was scared in the dormitory, too. I was scared every day after Papa went away. Wasn't no difference— most people are scared all the time, I think, anyway."

Antoine thought over his next question carefully. He was not sure if he should even ask. "When you are with these men do you ever enjoy it? Do you like it?"

"Oh, of course, sometimes. That's the times I feel like I'm a sinnin'. Mostly though, I just act as if it was wonderful while I think about doing my laundry or shopping for shoes down to Beasley's. But what about you, Antoine? Do you enjoy your time with other men? Is it any different from you and me?"

Antoine took a long time to answer. He wanted to explain himself to her as carefully and as truthfully as he could.

"Little Senora," he began. "Do you know what is a mule?"

"A mule? Yes, I know a mule when I see one. Horse with big ears."

"A mule is an unfortunate lonely animal. He is neither horse nor ass. He is barren and cannot produce young."

"Mules can't produce young?" Amber was curious. "Then where do baby mules come from?"

"They are the children of horses and asses and are unlike either—I am like that. I had a cherished friend that I was accused of doing things with that never happened. I was driven from my home because of that, and yet I have no feelings for the making of love to a woman. I fight men in the prize ring, and that is all. I admire women and yearn to protect them, and that is all. The sisters you met at Saint Agnes have a word for what I am. They say *celibate*. It is another way of saying mule. And that is what I am, and all I want to be—and that is all."

"But you said to me once that I might be able to do something for you. I thought—I don't know what I thought." Amber was puzzled.

"We will speak of that some other time. I am sleepy now and you must be too, but I will say, that what you might do for me sometime, has nothing to do with what you have done for others."

Antoine did not sleep that night. As the train rumbled through the darkness, his mind was filled with images of hungry, lonely girls. Whole dormitories filled with them—all alone—without hope—with no one to care for them, and with no opportunity to do better than just to stay alive.

How many? he wondered. *Where do they go? Is it worse when they are old? Homely? Does death just take them? Do they just disappear into loneliness and despair? Will Jesus—could Jesus blame them for just staying alive?* He knew the nuns at Saint Agnes would.

Chapter Nine

Upon leaving the train, Amber and Antoine found themselves in a nearly deserted depot on a hot August afternoon. Looking about, it would appear the town of Oceola was a deserted affair. A few horses stood by hitching rails scattered about. Their swishing tails and shaking manes, creating a vain effort to combat the summer plentitude of flies, provided the only signs of life along the street.

A small number of American flags, displayed from three or four store windows of what obviously served as the main street of the town, provided a scant bit of color to the bleak countenance of the settlement. Grudgingly permitted by a former slave-friendly territory, they were further a sign that the war was over, and the north had triumphed.

A well-worn sign, announcing the medical practice of Doctor Rueben Pritchard, hung above one of the windows a few doors away as the only clue that people actually lived here.

"What now, Antoine?" Amber wanted to know. "How do we find our way to your uncle?"

"I'm sure my Uncle Christof will not be hard to find. We were told he was quite prominent here.

What I need is for you to sit on one of these benches while I search out a livery. I do know his hacienda bears the name Twin Oaks. I am certain we will find him. It would have been better had he known we were coming."

"What if he's not glad to see us? See me?"

"He is family. My mother's brother. My Godfather. We will be welcomed, I am sure."

Amber was suddenly and quite visibly shaken. "But what will he think of me? Will he know what I am?"

"And just what are you?" Antoine asked, smiling.

"You know what I mean. Don't tease, Antoine. This is important. What if I am alone here…here in this Kansas?" She was at the brink of tears when Antoine took her hand. He pulled her to him and held her in a firm embrace that seemed to restore her demeanor.

"He will know that I am your protector, and you are my ward. And that you hold a place of honor in my heart. He will know that any love he has for me must be for you, also. As my ward, you are a part of family. Honor requires this among the Mendoza family."

"Mendoza?" Amber was puzzled. "Who?"

"I am Mendoza in Spain. In New Orleans, I am Acadia. Uncle Christof is Romero. And now that you are truly confused, you must let me search out a way for us to get from here to there."

"Christof Romero," she thought aloud. "Is there a wife?"

"She is Charlotte—I know nothing of her. She is from San Francisco—an American. Sit, wait. I must go now."

Totally bewildered and now more afraid than ever, Amber seated herself on one of the green wooden benches by the door of the depot. No sooner was Antoine gone from her sight, she had the terrible thought that he might not come back. To be left here alone was a terrifying thought. Perhaps she had trusted Antoine too much. She was becoming more anxious by the minute. Thirty minutes slowly passed.

At last she could stand no more. She sprang from her seat and ran to the edge of the plank sidewalk and, nearly in a panic, peered up and down the dusty avenue for any sign of Antoine. It was at that moment, she heard him call out, "Amber! Amber! Here! Here I am."

She turned and, from the opposite direction he had disappeared, he now was coming forward in a cabriolet buggy pulled by a matched team of black horses. The whole affair being driven by a large black man in a white coat and black silk top hat. Her heart leapt in her breast. Never had she been so glad to see anyone. He continually spoke to his team and affectionately called them by their names, Punch and Judy.

The buggy ride through a rural setting was a totally new experience for Amber. It was true that peering out of the train windows she had seen the first fields she had ever encountered. She had heretofore seen only the streets and avenues of a metropolis. Amber now found the openness and broad distances of space to be beautiful beyond belief, and at the same time a bit frightening.

"What are these fields?" she wanted to know. "What is that tall yellow grass?"

"See the grain heads at the top of the stalks? It is wheat. Winter wheat. The farmer sows the field in December, maybe November. Now in late summer, they will harvest it and turn it into flour and then into bread—for hungry little girls like you," Antoine teased.

"But, so much of it? It's like the Gulf of Mexico—only tan."

"Amber," Antoine corrected her, "like a sea of Amber."

Because of the heat, the team of blacks were not pushed very hard, and so the buggy made the five mile trip in less than two hours. Amber had never seen so much of rural America. It seemed to her its beauty could just go on forever.

Two hours in the summer sun though, and coupled with the long train ride, had made her sleepy. She was about to close her eyes for a nap, when Antoine exclaimed, "I think we're here. This is Twin Oaks!"

Amber opened her sleepy eyes to discover a long lane lined with willows and oaks leading up to the largest, most stunning house she had ever seen. It reminded her so much of the mansions in the Fontainebleau section of New Orleans, but larger, with far more landscaped grounds surrounding it.

Built in the Southern Colonial style, its two and one-half story façade stood stately above the Doric columned front porch. Two large picture type windows graced the first floor, each with timeless Romanesque arches draped across their tops to serve as classic lintels. At each end of the structure's first floor, slanted bay windows formed of prism-cut glass panes were arranged to catch the arc of the sun as it crossed the Kansas sky and bring the myriad of color and textures to the home inside.

The second story displayed four, evenly spaced windows with matching lintels and more of the beveled glass. Stark white against the green of the oaks and willows, the Twin Oaks household was a picture of peace, tranquility, and quality of the highest order.

"My God," Amber gasped, "are we to stay here?" She could not help but wonder what beauty lay within these white clapboard walls.

Antoine had once seen a drawing of this spectacular home that his uncle had sent to the family in Spain, but now, here in the present, it was far more impressive than he had remembered. The colored man in the white coat had removed their two bags from the rear of the cabriolet and stood waiting to offer his helping hand to Amber as she stepped down from the buggy.

"I'll be need'n a dollar for the ride, sir," he spoke to Antoine. Antoine gave him a five-dollar gold coin.

"I cain't no ways change this, sir. Have you got somethin' else?"

"I would have you keep the money, sir. I am almost sure to need your services again. I presume you are at the livery most days, and if I ask for you, what is your name?"

"I called Charles," the driver responded. "I 'preciate the money, sir. You need me, you just say at the livery, 'I need Charles'—I be right there. Ol' Charles, he at your service. Could you just tell me your name, sir?"

Antoine thought for a moment. Somehow *Antoine* seemed a bit much for the occasion. "Andy," he said. "Should I require your services again, I'll leave the name *Andy*." With that, Antoine and

Amber each picked up their single bags and began the walk up the long lane to the house.

A faint breeze found its way along the lane making the stroll a pleasant one, and Amber actually had begun to forego a bit of her tensions and find a bit of relaxation on the walk to the house. A few butterflies flitted about the several flower beds they strolled by, and a large goldfish pond drew them to its graveled banks. The flashes of gold within the pale green water betrayed the presence of the gilded denizens.

"Look—look there, Amber."

"Where?" Amber wanted to know. Then following his arm down to his pointing finger and out into the water, she at last saw what he was showing. A pair of colossal eyes seemed floating on the water's surface as an enormous bullfrog eyed the pair suspiciously. It was at this moment they heard the hailing call: "Haloo. Hey, there. Hellooo."

They turned in time to see an angular figure clad in faded bib overalls, a rumpled straw hat, and carrying a gardener's hoe emerging from a gigantic flower bed of rhododendron.

"Hello, there, can I help you folks?" The tall, wiry man approached them as he shed a pair of yellow work gloves. He removed the straw hat and mopped his thinning pate with a red bandanna. Antoine had encountered men of this stature before while in the prize ring. Thin—better described as lean and probably stronger than they appeared.

"We're here to see Christof Romero," Antoine answered. The thin man moved closer to Antoine and lowered his head.

"Mister Romero?" he asked. "Christof Romero? You want Christof Romero? Who are you, sir? May I ask?"

"His nephew, Antoine Mendoza. My friend and ward, Amber Juliardo. I've come to see my uncle." The man in the overalls replaced his hat and leaned heavily on the hoe. His sudden, downtrodden demeanor told Antoine at once there was something wrong—something amiss.

"You bein' his nephew and all, I hate to be the one atellin' you this, sir." He paused and sucked in a deep breath.

"What?" Antoine asked. "What is it?"

"Well, sir, Mister Christof—well, Mister Christof— he's been dead more'n three weeks now, sir." Stunned, Antoine retreated to a nearby wooden bench and slumped onto it. Immediately, tears filled his eyes and he stretched out his hand to Amber. Amber took his hand and slid onto the bench beside him.

"Oh, Antoine," she whispered. "Oh, my poor Antoine. So sorry. I'm so sorry."

"You bein' his nephew, how is it you didn't know 'bout it, sir?"

"I've been in New Orleans, away from the family a long time—I don't suppose Uncle even knew where I was. I should have let him know. I should have done something. What was it? How did he go?"

"Him and me was feedin' horses. I ain't the gardener here. I'm the livestock man. I was just helpin' trim up a little. Anyhow, Mister Christof and me were feedin'. He picks up a bale of hay and just sort of slumps to the ground with it. I get him up and he seems alright. We hitch up a buggy and I drives him into town to Doc Pritchard. Get him in Doc's office I do, and he slumps again—only this time he's gone. Never says a word—just gone."

"Oh Antoine, I'm so sorry for you. Is there anything I can do? Just say?" Amber held his hand against her cheek.

"My aunt?" Antoine asked. "Is my aunt here? Is she well?"

"Miss Charlotte? She ain't here this minute but she gonna be back real soon. We eat at five. She sometimes don't eat, but once a day. Supper though, she eats. She don't hardly eat much since Mister Christof is gone. Eats 'bout like a bird. But she'll be back from old Randall's house real soon. Randall's pretty sick and she's seein' to him. That's why I was gardenin'. Randall's the man does all this plantin'."

"I've never met her, I'd like to see her." Antoine's tone was subdued. Tears filled his eyes and Amber could not help but wonder what this turn of events meant for her.

"Let's get you up to the house. You and Missy Amber can rest in the parlor till Miss Charlotte comes. I tell my missus to set a couple more places for supper."

"Are you sure that'll be alright?" Antoine wanted to know.

"I know Miss Charlotte's gonna be glad you all are here. I know another thing, too. You gonna love your supper. My wife's a fixin' it right now and there ain't no doubt she's the best cook in this county."

Antoine looked to Amber. He thought she looked scared, troubled. He squeezed her hand a bit tighter. He hoped she was a bit reassured.

"Maybe we should go back to town," Antoine ventured. "We don't mean to inconvenience anyone."

"Was I to let you leave 'thout see'n' Miss Charlotte? Well, I just don't know what kind of a fit she'd pitch. Now you all come on." He picked up Amber's bag and started up the path to the house.

"I'm going to rely on your judgment—I just hope you're right. I would like to meet my aunt, though. We'll do as you say, mister. What's your name, sir? I didn't catch your name."

"I'm Ledbetter, sir. Oney Ledbetter. Call me Oney."

Chapter Ten

Once inside the house of Twin Oaks, Amber began to see beauty and stylish quality she had not encountered before. There were Oriental carpets, velvet drapes, overstuffed furniture, and gleaming polished wood. All was magnificent to Amber's limited experiences.

Oney Ledbetter led the pair into a room he called the sitting parlor and invited them to take a seat. As he vanished into the darkened depths of a wide hallway, Amber selected a highly polished rocker with cushioned seat and back of pink and white checkered chintz, while Antoine slumped onto a dark green, plushy upholstered love seat.

Amber studied the room as she steadily rocked in the chair constructed of various sized spindles turned from an elegant wood. There was a white, marbled fireplace here, a mirror of leaded and beveled glass there.

An elegant sideboard of mahogany graced one wall, its surface displaying an impressive collection of cut-glass bottles and decanters, with cups and stemmed glasses to match. The other furnishings of the room included a pair of small sofas with matching footstools, and a huge overstuffed seat near the fireplace that could be best described as an easy chair. Glancing now at Antoine, she could see that exhaustion of the day was overtaking him. He appeared nearly asleep.

Not so with Amber. Her excitement of discovering these new surroundings was somewhat overwhelming. Trying to take it all in at once, she sprang from her seat in the rocker and paced about the room. Pausing by a window, she parted the drapes which were strategically closed to keep out sunlight on such a warm day. She discovered she was staring down the lane that led to the dusty roadway.

She was so surprised to see a woman on horseback entering the lane from the road at a smooth, loping canter. The woman rode a tan horse. *No, more yellow,"* she thought, *not even yellow.* She mused, *Gold! It's a woman riding a golden horse.* The steed was indeed stunning to Amber. As gold as an October moon with flaxen mane and tail afurl, the horse was a gathered ball of energy prancing up the pathway as the rider pulled her horse to a slower gait.

Now Amber began to look at the rider. Clothed in black riding boots, a blue shirt with a tan vest, and a grey Stetson hat, she sat in the saddle as one who had ridden many times before. All in all, as

Amber looked upon the woman astride the golden horse, she thought, *Beautiful—they're just beautiful. Who could she be? Charlotte? Is that Charlotte?*

All at once, she noticed the woman had raised her face and was looking directly at her watching as she peeked through the parted drapes. Startled to be so discovered, Amber quickly jerked the drapes closed and swiftly retreated to the safety of her rocker.

Embarrassed to the core now, Amber felt her face flushing. She hoped against hope that the woman on the horse had not seen her peering between the drapes.

"Antoine, Antoine," she called. "Antoine, wake-up, I think your aunt is here."

The next several days were lost in a whirlwind of random emotions within the Twin Oaks mansion. For Antoine, there was the deep sadness of losing the uncle he had admired and loved since he was a boy. At the same time, there was the exhilaration of being so warmly welcomed by an aunt of such grace and charm and beauty.

Charlotte was at once delighted at the arrival of a nephew she knew of, but had no idea of ever seeing. She was, though, deeply troubled, as his visit brought back all the painful memories of the death of her husband. Further, she found she adored Antoine for his charm and masculinity.

Additionally, Charlotte was confused by the presence of this lovely young woman who seemed perpetually within the very shadow of Antoine.

What was she to him? she wondered. *And what is this old-world relationship called a ward? What is a ward anyway? A concubine—a lover?* She found Amber to be a fine, young, and interesting woman although her presence was somewhat cloaked in mystery.

For Amber, the whole experience was confusing, exhausting and wonderful. She had never been this close to this obvious abundance of everything.

That first afternoon, two more women came into the parlor an hour after Charlotte's arrival. They were quite different in appearance. One, a lady of medium build, seemed to Amber to be in her mid-thirties and was clothed in a dark blue, osnaburg linen dress with a starched, snow-white apron, her soft brown hair cut short in front and pulled to the back of her head forming a perfect bun. Her smile was large, and Amber thought sincere.

The other lady, obviously somewhat older, wore a similar costume, but her hair was long, reaching down to her shoulders. It had once been as black as the crow's wing, but now was shot through with silken stands of silver. Her complexion was two shades darker than Amber's.

"Antoine, Amber, these are two girls I could never do without. This is Maude Ledbetter," she said, indicating the youngest of the pair. "You've met her husband, Oney. Maude is our wonderful cook. I warn you, don't try to call her Missus Ledbetter, she'll tell you right quick she is Maudy." The cook gave a gracious little curtsy. "And our housekeeper who keeps things so orderly in our lives is named Sally, Sally Two Feather. Sally and her people were here long before Chrisser and I came along. Sally is a Wichita. We are very proud to have her friendship. Matter of fact, we're proud of them both. We love them like family."

"Chrisser?" Antoine asked. "You called my Uncle Christof, *Chrisser*?"

"Oh, yes I did," Charlotte responded. "We had funny names for each other. He was Chrisser, I was Charley."

"Wonderful!" Antoine exclaimed amid his laughter. "That's just wonderful." It was becoming more evident by the moment, the reasons his uncle had loved this fine and spirited woman.

"It's been a long and wonderful day," Charlotte lamented. "Sally Two Feather will take you, Amber, to a room for tonight. Antoine, please go up the stair, and the room on your right at the top will serve you for now."

It was the morning of the second day that Charlotte noticed Amber was dressed in the same clothing of the previous days.

"Amber, darling," she said, "would you like to put on something fresh? I'm sure it'll make you feel better—fresher."

"Oh, my bag with all my good clothes got lost. I think 'twas left on the train," she lied.

"Come with me. I understand that. I've left things on trains many times. It's such a bother." Charlotte led Amber down a long hall to her own first floor bedroom. Amber's first impression was of a very large room. It held a large four-poster bed and a scattering of sitting furniture.

A large window with open drapes displayed the huge rhododendron plant at the west end of the house where Amber had first seen Oney Ledbetter. Three full length mirrors and slatted doors to two large closets gave the impression of affluence. Brass sconces were mounted in pairs on each wall of the room. These held the oil lamps that would illuminate the chamber at night.

"Look here Amber," Charlotte said, opening one of the closet doors. "I think you and I are close enough in size you can wear any of these," she said, indicating the great closet's bountiful hangings of fashionable clothing for every occasion. "The other closet is mine, and this one can be yours."

Amber was visibly shaken by this lady's generosity to her. Gifts of any kind or value had been a sparse commodity in the life of Amber Juliardo. She began to tear up, slowly at first, and then to sob.

"Now dearie, you don't need to cry like that." Charlotte took Amber in her arms, and her gentle hug gave her a feeling of warmth and safety she had not known since her father had gone away.

Taking Amber by the hand, Charlotte led her through a doorway into an adjoining room. Though smaller, the room was appointed similarly to the larger one.

"Dear Amber," Charlotte whispered, "I'd like you to take this as your room while you're here. I'd like to have you near me. I've never had a young woman like you to share things with. This room—this room," Charlotte faltered, "this room was meant to someday be a nursery. It just was never needed. I want you to use it. I hope you'll stay a long time. I hope you and Antoine will stay a long time. I have things happening—serious things that I need help with. Please stay with me for a while, Amber. You'll understand soon, I promise—I promise."

It was at this moment that Amber spied something of great interest to her nestled in the corner of the room as if almost hidden.

"Charlotte?" she asked. "Is that a sewing machine?"

"Why, yes. Yes, it is. Do you know about sewing machines dear?"

"I've sewn a lot. Not on a machine like that, though. It looks so delicate."

"Come see, Amber." Charlotte was actually pleased with the change in the conversation's direction. "I've had it two years or more now. I intended to take up sewing. I thought myself to be a seamstress. I bought everything. Look at that chest." She indicated a large cedar trunk sitting next to the intricate mechanism. "Full up to the top with bolt after bolt of cloth, thread, needles and so on. Bought and never used. It's a good machine, too. Wilcox and Gibbs, they call it—made out in Rhode Island somewhere. Supposed to be better than a Singer."

Amber was gazing intently, drinking in every graceful line and curve of the contrivance.

It's so elegant, she thought. Not at all like the heavy-duty machines she had labored over so strenuously back in New Orleans. "Look how funny," she exclaimed to Charlotte. "They've made the treadle look like two footprints."

"It has a handwheel, too—for when you want to go very slowly. And it's single thread—makes a fine and tiny seam."

"Could I sew on it sometimes, Charlotte?"

"Of course, darling. Use it as you will. I have no further interest in it at all."

Amber eagerly looked forward to experimenting and sewing something with this remarkable appliance.

What shall I make first? she pondered. *What first?*

Chapter Eleven

The next few days, things seemed to Amber to move very slowly around the house and grounds. It seemed that Charlotte and Antoine were engaged in meeting after meeting. Amber was not in the least upset by being excluded from these as she regarded them as family business. To occupy herself and use the spare time she had on her hands when not at the Mister Wilcox Gibbs, as she had named the sewing machine, she began a serious exploration of the Twin Oaks grounds.

She remembered the gardener's name was Randall, and now she approached him as he knelt before a colorful display of snapdragons. He was carefully weeding the bed of the white and pink little oddities when Amber began to speak with him. Noticing his skin was approximately the shade of Sally Two Feather, she ventured, "I know your name is Randall, are you a Wichita, too? Like Sally?"

"Kiowa," he replied.

"Oh, I didn't know. Kiowa, is it? Are there other hordes here too?"

"Not hordes. Clans—bands—tribes—nations. Depends on how many. Kiowa is now only a clan.

All of our kind left for Texas years ago. Most are now Comanche. We have Choctaw, a few Cherokee, some Kansas. Lots of clans here."

"So all sorts of Indians were here? Long ago, I mean."

Randall stood up from his work. He liked this pretty little white girl. He liked that she was interested in him and his people.

"My grandfather told me that fifty years ago many hundreds of Indians—Indians of all tribes and nations lived here. Many—like stars—blades of grass. Buffalo were here. Some say more than two million. Where there are buffalo—Indians will be, too." Randall offered his hand, and Amber shook with the Kiowa gardener. Very curious now, she asked one more question.

"Randall, could I ask what your last name is?"

"Big Turtle," he replied. "I am Randall Big Turtle. The turtle is a peace sign. My family were Kiowa chiefs in peace time. Not in war. For many, many years we have grown things in the ground—corn, wheat, squash..."

"And snapdragons," Amber said.

"Yes—snapdragons," he answered.

That same afternoon, she encountered Oney Ledbetter at the door to the main stable.

"Come, Amber. Let me show you something. Something really special." At first Amber hesitated.

She, based on her past experiences, was at once suspicious of a man who would invite her into a dark place to show her something. Reflecting on her fears, she realized this was Oney Ledbetter. She was sure he could be trusted. Well, almost sure.

The barn was dim and smelled of clover hay. Oney led her to a stall, and she peered over the slatted fence. Once her eyes adjusted to the dimness, she realized she was looking at two dappled gray horses, one much larger than the other.

"These here are Percheron," he told her. "Finest draft horses in the world. Came from France many years ago. That knight, Lancelot, one who stole the lady Guinevere away from old King Arthur, rode one of these hisself, bein' a Frenchie as he were. You know, Maudy used to teach school, and she learned me all about that. Long time ago though, I reckon— ain't no more knights about, but we still got their horses."

"They're just beautiful." Both horses turned their intelligent faces toward the strange pretty girl. Their fox-like ears projected forward in a questioning manner.

"Little feller there—he's just seven months old. The big'un, she's fourteen months. Brother and half-sister they are. You see this pair when they two, three years old—they weigh two thousand pounds each, maybe more. Six-foot high at the shoulder. Tall as me. Takes a mighty horse to weigh a ton, Miss Amber. Ain't they just the bestest things you ever saw?"

"Don't they eat a lot? I'd bet so," Amber asked.

"One eats as much as two," Oney allowed, "but can do the work of four. Pretty special they are."

Amber agreed. They were magnificent. She wasn't sure she believed they would ever weigh a ton each, but she knew she liked Oney Ledbetter. She thought that anyone who could be so obvious in their love for animals had to be a pretty good sort. Leaving the barn, she was anxious to return to her sewing.

First, she made an apron. Then, a second apron, but with pockets. Next came a simple white shirt and a blue jumper. Following this, she wanted to try a peasant's blouse with puffy, short sleeves and an ankle length skirt. She was just rethreading the bobbin when she heard Charlotte's voice calling. She sensed this was another family meeting. Only this time she was included.

Chapter Twelve

It was a Sunday night following the splendid evening dinner prepared by Maudy Ledbetter when Charlotte determined the anticipated meeting was to happen.

Maudy had, indeed, fed everyone extremely well that evening. She had roasted a large pan of bobwhite quail harvested that very day by the shotgun of Oney Ledbetter and two English setter pups, Whiskey and Pistol. A cauldron of collard greens mixed with white and yellow hominy, and a large bowl of stewed apples, coupled with the warmth of the evening had everyone in a relaxed, comfortable frame of mind. Blackberry cobbler with thick cream from Jennifer the Jersey, along with hot, strong Arbuckle's chicory, settled the best meal Amber ever recalled having.

Oney Ledbetter had lighted the sconce lamps in the cozy parlor, and Sally Two Feather had set out a pitcher of sweetened tea, along with cut glass tumblers complete with muddled mint settled within their bottoms.

At about six o'clock, the room was beginning to shade a bit and some of the September heat was beginning to give way to forthcoming darkness.

Sally Two Feather, Maude, and Oney Ledbetter sat side by side on the greatest of the sofas. Amber was at Antoine's side on the loveseat, and Charlotte occupied the easy chair near the darkened fireplace. Maude, Oney, and Sally felt a bit uncomfortable at being invited to what was obviously a gathering where important family business was to take place. Amber was eager to learn just what kind of family business would be discussed and why she was there.

"Twin Oaks is a fine place," Charlotte began, "Don't we all agree to that?" The affirmatives were in unison. "I know Amber appreciates the beauty of Twin Oaks as I have seen her so diligently exploring every corner of the house and grounds."

"Oh my, yes!" Amber eagerly offered. "I've never seen anything like this place— this lovely place."

"And you, Antoine, what is your impression? I know that you came from beautiful surroundings back in your native Spain. How does Twin Oaks compare?"

"My dear Aunt Charley," he began.

"Oh! You've used your Uncle's pet name for me! I like that. I like that a lot."

"Well, Charley, it's gorgeous. There's nothing left to say."

"Oney," Charlotte said, "I don't want to embarrass you, but would you mind telling Amber and Antoine how you came to be here with us?"

Amber saw Oney was taken aback by the request. He swallowed hard. "No, I guess I don't mind if anybody's really interested. It ain't somethin' I'm proud of. But I ain't much ashamed either. I, well—I shot a man back in Louisville and we just had to leave—ended up here."

He swallowed again and resumed his tale. "I was trainin' runnin' stock at Red Horse farm. That's a big racehorse farm right near the Woodlawn track. That's where they run the two-year-olds, you know. We was so close I could see the judges' stand from our back porch. Well, I was workin' there, and one day I spot about three—four rats in the corn crib. Another hired hand on the place, Albert Gesselman, borrowed me his pistol and I went to shootin' at these rats. Well, I can tell you I ain't much of a rat shot—used up almost all the shells I did, and never did hit no rat. Not one, Ma'am." He paused and looked to Charlotte for guidance.

"Please go on, Oney. We need to hear this story—all of us. You're an important part of the Twin Oaks' story—you and Maudy and Sally." Oney wiped his forehead with the sleeve of his work shirt. The sun was just dimming but the room was still warm.

"Later that same day, I took a buggy to town to pick up Maudy at a store where she was workin' at," he continued. "She, me and her are walkin' back to the buggy when this feller, Jase Cox, happens along. I see he's kinda drunk, so I try to steer Maudy around him and he just, for no reason at all, just bumps her. Real hard like. I say, 'Watch out there, fellow,' and he hits me with his fist. So I hit him back. Pretty hard, I hit him, too. He falls on his back side and gets up with a pocketknife in his hand. I still had the pistol, so I pulled it out of my pocket and shot him with it. Weren't much of a shootin', I guess. Hit him in the foot, I did. Some said I shot off his great toe but I ain't for sure 'bout that. Anyhow, sheriff locks me up and next day this judge, Judge Coltrane it was, Judge Adam Coltrane says it's alright that I shot old Jase, what with him havin' that pocketknife and all. He says I'm innocent—lets me go right there—no fine nor nothin'."

"But," Antoine interjected, "If the judge said you were innocent, why did you have to leave? Give up your job?"

"Well, Jase—he's got all these cousins, you know an' uncles. They was just giv'n me and Maudy a hard time 'bout every day. Tore up Maudy's flower bed. Broke a couple of windows at our house. Left our pasture gate open. Now I got horses all over the Ohio River banks. Finally, I go back to my pal, Albert, and ask him can I borrow that pistol again. He says to me, 'You ought to get the heck out of here afore somethin' really bad happens.' Maudy says so, too. We get on a train headin' west and wound up here when our money ran completely out. Your uncle comes along the train stop—we sittin' on the sidewalk—he looks us over and 'thout another word says, 'Come on with me.' We been here ever since— 'bout seven or eight years now, I guess. We are here—I'd say, we're here because of a good man—a man we—me and Maudy loved a lot. That's how we here—'cause a good man brought us here. As for Miss Charlotte—well they's no finer nor grander lady. We owe her and your uncle everything."

"That's the whole story," Maudy Ledbetter added. "Finest folks in Kansas befriended us when we was in a real bad time."

Amber knew she liked Oney and Maudy from the first day she met them. Now she liked them even more.

"Sally," Charlotte said, "tell Amber and Antoine about Buffalo Man."

"Bad husband," Sally started, "whiskey— mean—say he's gonna cut my ears, like old time Kiowa. Mister Chris brings me here—long time now. Buffalo Man is gone—dead maybe. Hope so. I care for Mister Chris and Miss Charlotte. I have ears. Kiowa days long over. That is big true."

"I look at this place," Charlotte began in a dreamlike voice, "so beautiful. So much work went into this place—a work of love. There was nothing here when we first came. Only buffalo—hundreds buffalo—everything we tried to build, the buffalo crashed it down. And in addition to that, do you know what you always find when you encounter lots of buffalo?"

"I know!" Amber sang out. "I know. Indians! Whenever you have buffalo you have Indians, too. Randall told me that—Randall Big Turtle."

"Oh, Amber," Charlotte sang out, "you are so right! You've learned so much about this place since you've been here. Indians—Indians a plenty— Wichitas, Cherokee, Choctaw, Kickapoo—some Cheyenne and Kiowa, too. Most of them were just pesky—stealing stuff, riding through the gardens and vineyards. Just small stuff—'cept for the Kiowa. They could really be dangerous. Chrisser carried a gun everywhere he went—made me carry one, too. Kept a rifle back of the kitchen door. You're so right, Amber—we had buffalo and Indians alright. But let me make you aware of another problem. When you look out onto the open prairie, what's the one important thing you don't see?"

The Ledbetters exchanged smiling glances. They knew where Charlotte was going with this.

Antoine replied, "I don't know Aunt Charlotte. What's missing?"

"Yes," it was Amber now, "What is it? I think the plains are wonderful. I've never seen so much space."

"Yes indeed," Charlotte responded, "but look carefully. What you don't see are trees. There are no trees. How do you build a house like this with no lumber? How do you acquire lumber when you have no trees? These two great oaks were here when we arrived. Not another tree for more than twenty miles. Those willows that line our front lane were dug up from a creek bank way over in the Indian nation, and Chrisser and I hauled them thirty miles by wagon. Every board in this home was struck in an Arkansas sawmill, loaded on a railroad flatcar, and then hauled by horse and wagon from the train yard at Oceola here to this site. Three years—three years it took. Three years and hundreds of trips of slow-paced horses lugging overloaded freighters. Heat, rain, mud, cold. I was ready to quit a hundred times. Chrisser said, 'No, I promised you a home— and a home you shall have.'

"My Chrisser was an amazing man. He sailed around the Horn on the *Alexandria*, gathered up grape plants and cuttings brought to California by the Conquistadors two hundred and fifty years ago, married me, and we journeyed east to this place in Kansas. We passed at least three wagon trains of settlers headed west who thought we were crazy. One time, when the trip had grown so hard—I was so tired—I said to him, 'if you got rid of some of those plants we could travel easier'—he told me, 'these vines are the very blood of our dear Savior, Jesus the Christ. I will die before I foul them.' And I knew he would. He was a special kind of man."

"You remember the ship he came on? The *Alexandria*, was it?" Antoine wanted to know. "It's amazing you can recall that far back."

"Not at all," she reflected, "Alexandria is my mother's name. You see—I was there when he crossed the bar. I was my father's cabin boy. The *Alexandria* was my father's ship. I met your uncle aboard that vessel. We met and made that fearful journey together. We've never been apart since— well, until now. It's my mother that prompted this meeting. The Captain is long gone now. My mother is old—she is ill. Without Chrisser, I no longer care to be here. We must decide—all of us—what's to become of Twin Oaks. We must all carefully consider how to dispose of or utilize it in the best way."

"I am willing to leave the room while you talk," Amber spoke. "I am only here a short time."

"You most of all, Amber," Charlotte said. "I have come to love you as the daughter I wanted so badly but never attained. It is very clear to me that you and Antoine are one. No. You must be a part of it all. We must all, all of us, deliberate very hard. We'll meet again next Sunday—a week after that I'll be gone. I'll be gone, but you'll all still be here. Twin Oaks will still be here."

Chapter Thirteen

The second strategy meeting simply never took place. Amber, somewhat excluded now from the continuous conferences between Charlotte, Antoine, and Oney Ledbetter, continued her daily strolls around the grounds of Twin Oaks. She was aware things were being planned and discussed that would certainly affect her future, but she was also mindful of the fact that she was a guest at Twin Oaks and not a part of the controlling interest.

She daily called upon Randall Big Turtle and Sally Two Feather, if for no other reason than to say hello, to hear a voice other than her own. She continued her sojourn about the stables and sheds looking in on the Percherons and laying hens.

It was the windmill and the attached cattle tank that fascinated her the most. Beautifully painted glossy white with whirling, red and blue blades, it was a startling statement of color as it rose majestically above the flat of the plains. The attached metal tank was more than twenty-five feet across and a bit deeper than she was tall. Encircled with thick cable braces, it gave an impression of permanence and strength. Amber felt certain the whole apparatus played an important part in the ranch life of Twin Oaks. Her attention was called to the valves located at the bottom edge of the tank. *Must be the way it's drained*, she thought, and vowed to ask Oney more about the windmill and accompanying tank at her first opportunity.

It was later that same afternoon she discovered a twenty-acre fenced field. Randall would later tell her it was called the high meadow. To Amber it produced a tranquil scene where peacefully agraze, belly-deep in the green of abundant grass were nine, fine Black Angus cows, a few with rambunctious calves by their side.

There also was a magnificent herd bull. Knowing nothing of cattle, Amber nonetheless recognized this bull was something extraordinary. His massive neck, the curly hair that covered his face, along with enormous shoulders that exuded power and strength caused him to stand out magnificently against the cows with their inquisitive, feminine faces. Compared to the masculine presence of the herd master, the cows seemed almost delicate. Somehow though, she wasn't sure how, he reminded her of Antoine.

Amber finding ways to occupy herself, while conferences were rampant between Antoine and Charlotte, continued for about two weeks. And, of course, she sewed. Apron after apron and shirt after shirt, she made smocks, osnaburg trousers and even jackets. With each effort, the quality of her work showed marked improvement until, at last, her pieces were very nearly perfect.

When Randall Big Turtle's Aunt Minerva died, her sewing machine was brought by Randall to the mansion and placed in the sparse space still available in Amber's tiny quarters as a gift. A machine very different in operation to the machine she had named Mister Willcox Gibbs, it gave Amber an opportunity to learn even more about the mechanics and art of sewing. She named the machine the Texas Flyer after the train that had brought her to Twin Oaks.

Very early on one Monday morning, Amber observed that Oney Ledbetter and the team of Percherons had backed the farm's largest wagon up to the side door of the mansion.

In short order, Oney and Randall Big Turtle had the flatbed loaded with two steamer trunks and an assortment of leather and carpet baggage. Unsure of what she was supposed to do, Amber hid herself alongside of one of the big oaks, and watched as Charlotte seated herself alongside Oney, and the Percheron team drew them down the lane and onto the road, and slowly out of sight. In tears, she ran straight away to Antoine.

"She didn't say goodbye," she cried, burying her face into Antoine's chest. "How could she just go away like that? Not even a goodbye? Oh, Antoine, I love her so. Such a great lady. Is she gone? Do you think she's really gone?"

"She could not bring herself to say goodbye to us, Amber. So hard for her—so very hard. She walked to this spot—followed a team of oxen and walked along a wagon's side—walked with her "Chrisser" from San Francisco to here—this place. Right here. At least she can ride the Union Pacific back. Of course, we loved her. What's not to love? I know you thought a lot of her—what you may not know, Amber, is she thought a lot of you. But, as she said—she's gone. We're still here—Twin Oaks is still here."

"What does it all mean, Antione?" Amber said through her tears. "What does it mean for us—for you and me?"

"It means, sweet Amber—at last—at long last, you have your house."

–oOo–

What she had dreamt about for so long now seemed about to happen, and Amber found herself in a state of confusion. What to do next? How does one actually open and operate a bordello? And, after long deliberation, was it something she still wanted?

"Antoine," she asked, "Do you think I could ever be like Charlotte? I mean—could I ever be a real lady, a real gentlewoman like Charlotte?" Without waiting for an answer, she went on, "Antoine, do you think I'm pretty? Am I pretty enough that a man would come all the way out here from town to be with me?"

"Are you thinking of working again? I thought you were interested in the management—the operation of Twin Oaks. I thought you were finished in direct dealings with the customers."

"Oh, I am Antoine. I surely am. After meeting Charlotte, I would like to put that behind me— forever. I was just thinking though—until we get a couple of ponies—girls, I might have to carry us for a while."

"Let's not use the name *girls*. And drop the name *ponies*, too. I think of the young ladies who will work here as *hostesses*—*comperes*—*escorts*. I don't see our young women as *ponies* or *strumpets*—rather, lovely misses offering lonely gentlemen a few moments in the company of beauty and intelligence. That— perhaps, coupled with some physical enjoyment. That—Amber is the way I see our prospective commerce."

"Hot damn!" Amber exclaimed. "My Lord, Antoine, you are really full of shit! But I like it, Antoine. I like it a lot. I love it!

"Another thing I like is you keep saying *us* and *our* and *we're*. Am I to assume we're partners?"

"Would you like us to be?"

"Of course, Antoine. I'm so used to you now that I could never see myself without you. But, I would like to know how you took control of this property—this house—Charlotte's house?"

"We can get into that later, but for now I'll be leasing you the house. Your house money—the money you so closely guard—how much do you have?"

Embarrassment crept across Amber's pretty face. "Not very much, I'm afraid. My money looked a lot bigger on the streets of New Orleans than it does here at Twin Oaks."

"How much?" Antoine demanded.

"A hundred–and–sixteen dollars."

Antoine turned away and buried his face in a faked cough to disguise his amusement.

"It is well enough," he declared when he had composed himself. "I will give you a lease for an undetermined length of time, and you will surrender to me one–hundred–and–sixteen dollars."

"What of Oney and Maude?" Amber asked, "What of Sally and the workers?"

"All are mine to deal with," Antoine answered, "except for Sally Two Feather. She will help you with the required housekeeping and laundry. Once the bordello is in operation, you will pay her wages. Agreed?"

"Agreed," she replied. Amber turned on her heel and went straight away to her room to bring forth the house money. She had long suspected that she had a rare and beautiful friend in Antoine Acadia. Only now did she know how deeply that friendship truly ran. Amber had never considered that she might someday have a partner. But she knew she had one now. She could not have been more pleased.

The next ten days were a whirlwind of activity in the household of Twin Oaks. Amber hurriedly scurried from room to room, trying to visualize the kind of activities each would be suitable for.

Antoine and Oney erected and reconstructed a large bar they had rescued from an old defunct tavern in nearby Haverford. The carved, old fashioned woodwork of the antique bar proved astonishingly beautiful after an immaculate cleaning and polishing by the pair. It sat gleaming and seemed completely in place at the right side of the stone fireplace in the north wall of the expansive living room.

Next, three poker tables were added to the living room along with a field craps table. Amber was not intentionally setting up a gambling hall, but she had learned that successful bordellos often provided their guests with gaming opportunities and beverages, some even with elaborate menus as an extra source of income.

Still, the haunting absence of prospective hostesses, as Antione referred to them, was a leading problem. As she sat alone in the living room contemplating all of the new improvements coupled with the lavish surroundings, she began to dwell on how these new accoutrements compared with the squalid life she had left behind in New Orleans. It was at that moment she realized the solution for working girls had been with her, at least partially, all along.

"Antoine! Antoine!" she called. "Can you come in here?" Her voice was high pitched and frantic, causing Antoine to hurry to her side.

"What's the matter?"

"I want you to leave! To go right way! At once," Amber fairly shouted.

"And where is it I'm going? At once? Right away?" he shouted back.

"Back to New Orleans," she cried. "Back to my two best friends, Yvonne and Claudia. We all started on the street together. They'll be perfect. I'm sure they'd give their eyeteeth to work in a place like this. Leave the streets. Really have a home for a change. Please go, Antoine. Fetch them here for me. For *us*."

"That's a pretty long journey, Amber. Couldn't we just send for them?"

"Dear Antoine. That would never work. They would never have the money for train fare."

"Money is no problem. I could easily wire them the money they'd need."

"Money *is* a problem," Amber corrected him. "If you sent them money, whatever whoremaster, pimp, they were with at the time would have it away from them in an instant, leaving them barely enough to get drunk on, which they would promptly do. Besides that, they would never have the courage to board a train alone. They're just like I was a few weeks ago, Antoine. I could never have climbed on that train if it were not for you. You can bring them here, Antoine. If not for you, they'd never make it."

"You speak of them getting drunk— are you sure about this?"

"Once they are here—once they see this place— once they know you are on guard for them. When I tell them about Charlotte—once I try to *be* Charlotte for them—you'll see, Antoine, they'll be fine. They'll be perfect."

Two days later, still not completely positive the trip was a good notion, Antoine made arrangements with Oney to drive him to the depot. Armed with only a small leather valise that had once been his Uncle's, there was no need for the Percheron team and large wagon. Oney had hitched a prim little mare called Junebug to a simple, shafted, but covered buggy. Amber watched from the front porch as they made their way out of sight along the dirt road that led to town.

"A few more days," she thought aloud. "A day or so—or ten maybe. We'll have ponies." She was more excited than she had been in a very long time. The thought of regrouping with her old comrades quickened her pulse, and she distinctly felt a butterfly in her stomach.

"We'll be in business!" she cried aloud. It was then she noticed Randall Big Turtle. He was weeding a bed of peonies at the opposite end of the porch as he readied them for fall.

"Hey, Randall," she called as loudly as she was able, "better get yourself ready—we gonna have hostesses!"

She turned and disappeared into the shady maw that was the doorway to the house. Randall leaned on his rake and removed his straw hat. He attempted to wipe sweat from his brow with his kerchief but there was none. November cool was already upon Kansas.

"What the hell was she saying?" he asked the flower bed. *"Hostess*? What's a *hostess*?"

Chapter Fourteen

The days awaiting Antoine's return with old friends, Yvonne and Claudia, were agonizing for Amber. She fully expected their return within a week. Now, on the fourteenth day of waiting, her anxiety was beginning to look more like worry.

She stalked from room to room of the mansion. She no longer explored the carefully manicured grounds that she so adored. A bitter November wind had brought early winter to Kansas and walking about outside had become formidable

No longer able to sit still long enough to enjoy her sewing, the two machines sat still and quiet. If she sat at all, she preferred to be alongside the stone fireplace in the living room. Oney Ledbetter kept a small, but warming flame kindled for her, and Maude kept the tea kettle aboil and the mixture of leaves that Amber liked at hand.

Wednesday late afternoon, it was Sally Two Feather who was the first to see the buggy belonging to Charles from the livery stable in town approaching with the two black mares, Punch and Judy. She could tell the two-seat buggy was filled with driver Charles in his top hat, and passengers huddled together in the rear seat, warding off the chill as best they could.

"Miss Amber! Miss Amber!" she called. "Company comin'. Mister Charles—he fetchin' company!" Ignoring the November air, Amber, filled with delight and enthusiasm, bounded out the mansion's front door and ran as hard as she was able down the lane to meet the buggy turning in from the road.

"Claudia! Yvonne!" she called. "Oh, my word. My Lord, I'm so glad you're here." She noticed the absence of Antoine instantly, and assumed he had stayed in town for one reason or another and would be coming along later.

Once inside the home, wraps removed, and following the exalted praises lavished on their new surroundings, the entire rest of the evening was filled with hugging, hot chicken and noodle soup, and generally catching up. A thought struck Amber. "Did either of you pay Charles for the buggy trip from the station to here?"

Claudia was quick to reply, "I had money— Antoine gave us money. I offered to pay him before we got into the buggy. He said he was already paid. He said Andy already paid him. Who's Andy?" Smiling, Amber remembered her first meeting with Charles, and Antoine giving him the gold piece.

"Speaking of Andy," Amber said, "I'm supposing Antoine stayed in Oceola for the evening? Is he coming tomorrow?"

Yvonne and Claudia looked each to the other. "We thought you knew about that, Amber. Though, when I think about it, there was no way you could have known, I guess."

"Knew what?" Amber sensed from the behavior of the two something was amiss. "Knew about what?" she repeated.

"Jail," Claudia said, "Antoine's in jail. New Orleans—Saint Anne's jail."

"Jail? What the hell are you talking about?"

Yvonne had begun to cry. "We was already on the train—Just sittin', talkin', waitin' for the train to start up. This man—this Parish Constable—he just walks up and says, 'Stick out your hands, Antoine.' He just puts handcuffs on Antoine and takes him right off the train."

Claudia continued, crying, "Antoine—he says, 'What for am I goin' with you?' Constable, he says, 'Killin' Daniel Ricardo.' Antoine say, 'I don't kill no Daniel Ricardo. He's alive when I seen him last time.'

"Constable says, 'Bullshit! You hit him so hard caved his head right in.' He takes him away right then. Vonnie and me starts to follow them off the train, and this constable says, 'Sit your ass down.

129

You all just stay right on this here train and don't ever let me see you back in Orleans no more.'"

"I swear, Amber, I thought you must have got a wire or somethin'. I really thought you knowed." Yvonne was sobbing uncontrollably now.

"Antoine could not have killed Daniel—are you even sure he's dead? Antoine told me he had some word with Daniel and when he left him, he was fine."

"He's dead for sure," Yvonne tried to speak through her crying. "I knowed him—He called on me a time or two. I knowed here for a month or two he's dead. Had a funeral over near Saint Agnes. Didn't go, but I sure knowed it was Daniel. He's dead all right. Antoine must have just lied to you, Amber."

"God damned men," Claudia added. "'Bout all they do is lie."

This turn of events took all the exuberance from the formerly delightful evening. With nothing left to say, each was ready to assume the bedstead to escape an exhausting and relentless day.

Sally Two Feather showed Claudia and Yvonne to the rooms Amber thought would make them most comfortable.

Amber climbed into her feathery nest and pulled the downy quilts up to her ears. Her bed was warm, welcoming, and soft, and her body, exhausted as it was, sorely needed it. But Amber did not sleep. No rest was to come her way this night. Her every thought was of Antoine and Daniel Ricardo. Her tears flowed freely when she thought of Antoine being in jail.

She supposed, after hearing the accounts given by Claudia and Yvonne, that Daniel Ricardo was surely dead. That seemed an undeniable fact. Amber knew another fact just as reliable. Antoine would never have lied to her.

–oOo–

It was just after nine the next morning when Sally Two Feather looked in on Amber.

"You awake, Miss Amber? It's after nine. You need to be up now."

"I'm awake—just layin' here," Amber yawned. "Just don't want to get up yet."

"I know, but you need to be stirrin'. United States Federal Marshall is here to see you this mornin'."

"Federal what? Marshall? What in hell are you talkin' about Sally?"

"I'm sayin' Grady Cole. The marshall. He's here askin' for you. I put him in the parlor, but you better be gettin' down there. I've knowed Marshall Cole a long time, and he's pretty much all business."

"Get him a coffee or somethin'. I'm up now—be right down."

Amber tried to imagine all sorts of things as she hurriedly dressed. What could a marshall be here to see her for? Was it about Antoine? Could it have to do with Daniel Ricardo?

She was expecting a no-nonsense, gruff individual like every other lawman she'd ever had occasion to encounter. As she passed the front door, she glanced out and discovered a handsome black horse, mounted with a western saddle, fixed to the hitching post. Distressed at meeting with a policeman, any policeman, she was fully expecting to be demeaned and disgraced. It had all happened before. What would this Grady Cole turn out to be? She carefully assessed him as she entered the room.

Tall and on the thin side, here was a ruggedly handsome man dressed in a pale gray uniform and holding a dark gray hat in his hand. A silver star was pinned to the left pocket of his shirt front. His trouser legs were neatly tucked into black, leather riding boots with small equestrian spurs attached. A wide black leather belt supported a large pistol at his waist.

A thick black comma of hair fell over his left eyebrow. The hint of a five o'clock shadow gave him a distinctly masculine appearance that Amber found more than a little appealing. Appealing or not,

Amber had little to do with lawmen that had ever been considered favorable. Her suspicions were acute.

"What did you want—Marshall, is it?"

"Are you Amber Juliardo?" No one had used her last name for so long, hearing it now took her aback a bit.

"Yes, I am Amber."

"Well, Miss Amber—is it Miss?"

"It's Miss, or just Amber."

"Well, Miss Amber, I'm here to see about a couple of things really. First off, I just last night got a wired message from a constable way down in New Orleans. Seems that big fellow that's been here with you for a month or two—that Antoine Acadia—been arrested down there and charged with murder."

"Antoine? A month or two? Have you been watching us?"

Grady Cole shifted his weight and went on, "Chris and Charlotte were close friends of mine. Good people. I've been keeping an eye on the place ever since Chris died. You and the big fellow included. Anyway, this constable knows you're here, too. He wants to know if you know anything about this killing."

Amber felt trapped. This country-cowboy policeman had cut through the small talk, and hit her with terms like 'murder' and 'killing'. She felt unsteady on her feet. Her mind was racing, searching for noncommittal ways of answering.

"I don't know about any murder," she lied. "Who got killed?"

"Kind of a local bad boy, I'd guess. Fellow named Daniel, Daniel Ricardo. You know him, do you?"

"Yeah. He asked me to marry him once." All of this seemed so very far away and buried so very deep in the past to Amber. She could hardly believe she had ever known a Daniel Ricardo. Loved him— was betrayed by him.

"So, do you think this Antoine could have killed him?"

"Certainly not!" Amber shot back. "And I have no idea who could have killed him."

"You don't seem very upset about him being dead. What with him wanting to marry you and all. You real close to this Antoine fellow, are you?"

"Antoine and I are partners. I love Antoine as a brother. I have nothin' to do with this. Neither does Antoine."

"Well, this constable—I'll wire him back what you've said. Even though, he may want to call you back as a witness."

"Would I have to go?" Amber was perplexed.

"I'm not really sure about that. Do you know Emil Gagnon?"

"No; who is he?"

"Lawyer fellow—got an office in town right next to the depot. Were I you, and if you hear more of this anytime, I'd see him about it before I did anything."

"You think I need a lawyer?"

Grady patted the Colt pistol holstered at his side. "Lawyers are like guns. You might never need one, but it's damn sure nice to know where there is one. Oops, excuse my language."

"I'll remember."

"Brings me along to another matter. Okay if I sit, Miss Amber?"

"Oh—sure. Sit please. Sit."

Grady eased himself onto the rocker and continued, "This wire I got from this New Orleans' constable—this Homer somethin'; I don't recall his last name. Anyhow, he knows these two girls you brought out here. Knows what kind of business they were into—knows all about them. Says he knows you, too. He's thinkin' you girls all getting together sounds like you might be tryin' to start yourselves up a business or somethin'. Maybe openin' a red lantern house, a sportin' house, as it were."

"If that *were* true," Amber wanted to know, "is there a law against it?"

"Well, what you need to know, I guess, is that I'm a United States Federal Marshall. There ain't another badge within forty miles of here. It's true I'm here to enforce the laws, but what's more important is I'm here to keep the peace. Since the war, Kansas ain't what you'd call a peaceful place, specially right here on this railhead. We have them all—Wild Bill Doolin, Sam Starr, the James gang, and all these big herds of cattle comin' to markets. Cowboys, Oklahoma bad men, renegade Indians. Keepin' the peace can get downright trying around here. And as for enforcing the law, I've never been able to keep a cowhand from looking for a woman. So, that being said, we have need here for a sportin' house—but it's going to be what I say it is."

"You can't bring yourself to just say 'whorehouse' can you?"

"I could. I'd rather not."

Amber tensed as she demanded, "Get to it, Marshall. What do you want here? You lookin' for a cut of the money? Maybe a little free time with the girls?"

"Maybe you better get a handle on who you're talkin' to, Miss Amber. I only got two goals in my life. To be a good man is first. Then, to be a good badge. We had a red lantern here before. Place called Julian's. 'Bout four miles on down the road. Cowboys go there lookin' for some funnin'. Then I find 'em along the road all beat and bloody. Horse, saddle, money all gone. Four, maybe five of those girls go to town together. Sellin' it right on the street. Pokin' fun at the town women. When I decide to stop it, trouble comes. I finally have to go out there and shut it down. When it's over, one of the girls is dead and two of them manager fellows shot up pretty good." Amber was captivated.

"No, I ain't wanting your money. I ain't for funnin' with your girls, neither. But if you want to operate here, I better not hear of a cowboy losin' his poke. He better be ridin' out on the same horse and saddle that brought him in. Any fist fighting or shooting takes place here; you're done".

"Your ladies want to shop in town, they go alone, one at a time. No showin' off on the street. Stay clear of the two churches and 'specially the school. Doc Pritchard is going to be out here every ten days to look things over. You know why, I'd expect. You're going to pay him for his services. You do these things the way I tell you, and you ought to make some money here and do pretty well with your red lantern. Am I pretty clear on that, Miss Amber?"

"You just can't bring yourself to say 'whorehouse' can you?" Amber said again.

Grady chose his words carefully. "Sure, I could…if I wanted to. I think that term's a bit degrading. Kind of low-down talk. You should understand, I'm not here to judge you, shame you.

And I'm not here for your money. I know you're like another thousand other young women here today — just tryin' to keep livin'. No place to go and no one to look after you even a little. The war just took way too many men — left way too many women with way too little. I'm just saying if you'll do it my way, you can go ahead. Any trouble though — just once, and you're out of business."

Amber found herself without words. Was this an honest policeman? Was there really such a thing?

"I'm clear, Marshall."

"I don't imagine it would do you no good to worry much about that Antoine fellow," he said, as he made his way to the door. "They'll probably just hang him in a week or so. Probably never get back to you once I tell them you don't know anything." Without another word, Grady Cole strode out the front door, mounted his saddle horse, and trotted off in the direction of town.

As Amber watched him depart, she had two distinct thoughts. As tough and direct as he was, she liked this Grady Cole. She must go to Antoine.

Chapter Fifteen

Amber knew it was time for a serious talk with Claudia and Yvonne. She was a little concerned about Yvonne. There was nothing she could put her finger on exactly, but there was a dreamy sort of sadness about her. She had never displayed such a melancholy before. Quite the opposite, Yvonne had always been a cheerful addition to any assemblage regardless of the occurrence.

Amber had observed her on several occasions staring out of one of the mansion's windows, seemingly at nothing, just gazing over the plains.

"Sally," Amber called, "please fetch Claudia and Yvonne for me. I'll wait in the living room."

"Yes, Ma'am," Sally's voice was faint as she was somewhere deep within the house.

Amber made herself comfortable in the old rocker. As she waited, her eyes wandered over the changes Antoine and Oney Ledbetter had made: the bar, the gaming tables. She wondered now, without Antoine, if they would ever be used.

"Oh, Antoine!" she cried aloud. "My wonderful friend. How will I ever live without you?"

Claudia flounced into the room with her usual jovial demeanor. Although it was three in the afternoon, she was clothed in a cozy-looking, flannel night shirt and carpet slippers.

"Are you ready for bed?" Amber asked.

"No—I'm ready for some laundry," she exclaimed. "I came here without very much to wear, and let me tell you my clothes are getting pretty high! The dog won't play with me anymore! It's wash day in Kansas, sister. Little Claudia's cleanin' up."

"Take yourself some clothing from Charlotte's old closet. There's a lot left in there. Take what you want."

"Oh, great! Thanks, Amber. Do you have anything needs washin' though?" Amber shook her head.

"Yvonne?" Amber asked.

"She'll be here soon. Not movin' too fast these days. Guess you know that, though."

"Know what?" Amber wanted to know. "What's wrong with Yvonne anyway. She's all droopy and sad like. What is it?"

"Are you sure you ain't figured it out, Amber?"

"Figured what out, Claudia? What's going on here?"

"Knocked up," Claudia said. "Figured you could see by her ways. Belly ain't showin' yet, but her sadness is."

"I'm here," Yvonne announced from the doorway, startling both Claudia and Amber. "It's time I told you the truth, Amber—I'm not any good to you. I wasn't goin' to come here but, Amber, I had nowhere to go. I'm going to have a baby, Amber." She broke into tears and heavy sobs. Amber was at once stunned and compassionate for one of her oldest friends.

"Oh, Yvonne, my dear Vonnie, you were right to come here. We love you Vonnie, Claudia—Claudia and me. We can help you. It'll be alright. Don't cry. Please, Vonnie, don't cry."

"You bet!" Claudia chimed in. "The Saint Agnes Trio. You got caught, Yvonne, but you have to know it could have been me—or Amber."

Amber took Yvonne in her arms and held her closely. She tenderly brushed Yvonne's hair from her face. Fishing a lace kerchief from her pocket, she dabbed at Yvonne's tears.

"Antoine," Amber said, "Antoine will be back soon. You'll see. He'll help care for you, too."

At this, Yvonne leapt back, freeing herself from Amber's embrace. Nearly collapsing now in tears, she rushed from the room leaving Amber astonished.

"What was that about?" Amber managed. "What set her off like that?"

"Who would you think was the father of that baby?" Claudia asked. "Why do you think the mention of Antoine would horrify her like that?"

"Horrify? What the hell are you talking about, Claudia? Antoine cares for all of us—best friend we've ever had."

"Yeah, and he killed Yvonne's lover, too. He was her future husband as well as the baby's father." Claudia's words seemed to freeze in her throat.

"Sort this out for me." Amber was more than baffled. "First of all, Antoine has killed no one. But just tell me who he is supposed to have killed."

Claudia lowered her eyes. "Daniel Ricardo," she managed.

"Ricardo!" Amber was aghast. "She was about to marry Daniel Ricardo? Is this a joke? This cannot be for real. The baby is his? Oh, my God!"

Claudia went on, "So you see, Amber—when you mention Antoine—and he's the one what killed…"

"Antoine killed no one," Amber argued. "That's bullshit—just bullshit!"

"How do you know he didn't do the killing. He's in jail for it. Everyone thinks he did it 'cept you. Why do *you* think he didn't?"

"He told me so!" Amber was nearly yelling now. "Antoine would never lie to me, Claudia! Never!"

Now it was Amber speaking through her tears. "How could Yvonne ever have anything to do...How could she get herself involved with a snake like Daniel Ricardo?"

"How did you? How did I?" The question struck Amber in the pit of her stomach.

"You too, Claudia?" Tears streaked Amber's cheeks. Claudia was thoughtful. She took a long time to answer.

"Sure. Why not? He was there. He had money in his pocket, money I needed. Not that I thought about buying anything. I just wanted enough of his money that when I went to bed, I wouldn't be too hungry to sleep. It's that way every day for women like us, Amber, we have nothing—no one to say to us, 'Don't touch that stove. It's hot! Be home before dark! It's dangerous out there'. No one watches out for us. No one to catch us when we fall. If we fall, it's all the way—no bottom. Babes in the center of the wolf pack. As for men, everyone we meet has a plan for us. Except, it's not for us—never for us!"

She went on, "I have a shrimper boyfriend I see sometimes. He says he's afraid when the boat gets caught in a storm. We, you and me, we are in the storm every day. We are children of the storm—you, me, and Yvonne—now Yvonne's having a baby. If it's a girl, the storm will have another child just like us, Amber. Just like us." Amber was plunged into sadness with the unbridled truth of Claudia's words.

"Oh, Claudia! I can't talk anymore. I'm just lost right now. Yvonne, Antoine—it's too much—too much."

"Amber, please listen to me," Claudia entreated. "We can work this out. I know we can. We're pals and we've been through hell together. No use talkin' 'bout Antoine anyhow, him being in jail and all. Let's get a night's sleep and try to sort this out in the morning." Claudia, in her inherent shrewdness, sensed it was time to rest this conversation, as it was obviously headed toward passion, rather than reason.

"Good night, Amber. Please—don't worry. We're too...too... Well, let's let it lay for now. We can talk more tomorrow when we...we..." Her voice faded away. She walked through the living room entrance and disappeared into the bowels of the darkened mansion.

Amber resumed her seat in the old rocker. She sat there a long time. She had elected never to tell Yvonne that Daniel Ricardo had proposed marriage to her, too. It could only hurt Yvonne more and serve no meaningful purpose whatever. Besides, she likely knew it anyway. Just like Claudia.

Mostly, she thought of Antoine. The contemplation of him sitting in a New Orleans jail moved her to tears, and she cried softly to herself. Eventually, she was taken by thoughts of action. She could no longer sit around and mope for Antoine. She needed to go to him. He needed her and she was sure of that. She was also sure that if it were reversed, and she needed him, he would be at her side in an instant.

"Sally! Sally Two Feather," she stood and called. Sally was not far away. As was her custom when there was important discussion taking place within her domain, she managed to be close enough to hear at least some of it.

"Yes, Ma'am, Miss Amber," Sally was in the room at Amber's side.

"You tell Oney to have me a buggy ready about eight o'clock tomorrow. Tell Maudy I'm takin' a trip, and for her to see to Yvonne and Claudia till I get back. Go on now. If you have to wake 'em up, do it, but I want that buggy—now shoo—hop to it." Without an answer except for a vigorous nod, Sally Two Feather hurried out of the room to complete her mission.

Amber walked to one of the front windows and gazed out at the darkness. She had no idea what she would encounter back in New Orleans. The idea crossed her mind that she herself might end up arrested. After all, she was Antoine's partner. Only two things she was sure of. She had to try. And she knew Antoine would never lie to her. He told her that he had left Daniel Ricardo alive, and she knew it was true.

Chapter Sixteen

In the early morning light, as Amber was at work preparing for her forthcoming journey, Claudia slipped into her room and sat beside her at her dressing table.

"Are you truly returning to Orleans?" Claudia ventured.

"Of course," Amber was hasty with her reply. "What else is there to do? I must go to Antoine."

"I worry about you is all. I worry the constable could arrest you, too. I worry—well, honestly, I worry about *me*, too—me and Yvonne. What should we do if you don't come back? We're strangers here. I don't even know where the hell Kansas is."

"If I didn't make it back, well, you'd be alright. Oney and Maudy would look after you. But don't you worry about it. I'll—we'll be back. Once I explain that Antoine is innocent, we'll be coming right back here."

"Good Lord, Amber, do you really believe that? Do you actually think that you can just tell that constable that Antoine told you that he didn't kill Daniel, and they'll just turn him loose—send you and him back to Kansas?"

"I'm ready for it to be a little tougher than that, Claudia. But whether I believe it or not, it's the thing I must do."

Claudia took a long time before speaking again. "Is there something romantic between you and Antoine? I mean—well isn't he—well, isn't he queer? I mean isn't he...?"

"He is what he is!" Amber snapped. "I do love Antoine, as I love you, as I love Yvonne. Going to help him is not a matter of love. It's the right thing to do. It's what he would do. If you needed him, Claudia, he'd be right at your side. I have to go. Whatever happens just happens."

"If that's your final word on the subject, when you get to Orleans remember the name 'Julio Esparza'."

"Who?" Amber asked.

"Esparza—Julio Esparza."

"Who is he?" Amber was intrigued.

"One of my regulars," Claudia answered. "I've seen him every payday night for more than a year now. He's a very dear boy—not bright, you know, but a dear boy, and the person who found Daniel's body on the docks. When you find him, ask him about the two Creole men."

"What Creole men? What are you getting at, Claudia?"

"He talked to me about it. He'd never found a dead person before—though heaven knows why not. There's a killin' on those docks three, four times a week. Anyhow, he's all excited about going to the docks and seeing the body. He wants to talk about it. He said he almost got fired by the constable for not arresting these two young Creole men who were the ones who told him about the dead man on the dock.

"He said they couldn't have had anything to do with the man's death, else they would not have come to him to report it. Maybe that's true. But I thought about it a lot. I said before, he's a dear boy. Not bright. When you get there, you look him up. Try Fat Boy's Pool Hall first. It's on Second Street. He's a real good pool shooter. Hangs out there a lot. Be careful if you have to go in there. Place is full of creeps.

"Soon as you have a chance, buy yourself a gun, Amber. I have a U.S. revolver that only cost about three or four dollars, but I don't go around places like Fat Boy's without it. Get a thirty-two, not a twenty-two. You want to know about Daniel Ricardo's death? Julio is the best place to start. Better you start with him than with the constable. If you're smart, you'll find Julio *before* you visit Antoine in the jail. I'm still thinkin' once you get into that jail, you might not be getting out."

Oney Ledbetter assisted Amber in mounting to her seat in the shafted buggy. He had harnessed the sorrel mare knowing she was one of Amber's favorites. He had raised the buggy's fabric cover to ward off the morning dew. He tried to engage Amber in cheerful, morning conversation to no avail. Her mind was awhirl, and she was deep in thought as she contemplated Antoine, Daniel Ricardo, Yvonne's baby, and now a new name for her to consider, Julio Esparza. She and Oney made the five miles to the train depot in an uncomfortable silence.

The train trip was long and uncomfortable. Amber's concerns for her friends and herself had kept her awake for nearly the entire trip, and pictures of Antoine locked in a jail cell tortured her constantly. By the time the train had reached New Orleans, she was in a daze.

She exited the depot to an overcast morning and a light drizzle of November rain. The cold drops of rain on her face seemed to revive her a bit, and she started telling herself it was time to come to her senses and alertness. Not knowing what lay ahead of her, she needed to be in control of her wits.

She began to walk away from the station and at the same time look for a carriage she might hire. The gloom and dampness of the morning had resulted in most carriages being hired by other disembarking train travelers, and Amber soon found she had walked more than three blocks without encountering a single buggy for employ.

The rain had become more intense, and she had ducked into a doorway to gather her senses and escape the dampness for a moment. She was dabbing the moisture from her face when she spotted the sign across the street from her shelter. There it was, *Fat Boy's Pool and Billiards. Candy. Drinks and Papers.* She knew it was far too early in the day for a pool hall to foster very much activity, and she needed a place to rest, collect herself, and while away the hours until a more appropriate time to look in on the pool room. At that moment, a vacant buggy for hire appeared out of nowhere, and she quickly hailed the driver. In a moment, she found herself comfortably seated in a dry, covered buggy seat warmed by a woolen lap robe.

The Princess Hotel was not elaborate, but perfectly clean and comfortable enough for Amber's short stay. At least she hoped it would be short. A short, fat bell boy in a livery a size or two too small carried the suitcase she had borrowed from Charlotte's closet down the hall to a room on the first floor.

She tipped the boy twenty-five cents, and then closed and locked the door behind him. Unaccustomed as she was to having money, Antoine had seen to it, after she had given over to him her house money, that she had a generous monthly allowance. With no place to spend money at Twin Oaks, she now was comfortable enough for a trip like this one. She had a leather money belt—also previously Charlotte's—that she wore under her clothing and it was a source of security to her.

She hung her damp clothing over the backs of two straight wooden chairs to dry and removed her shoes and stockings. She stashed her bag in the provided chifferobe and, still in her chemise, she gratefully stretched herself out onto a soft and comfortable bed.

After sitting for the long train ride, and the sleep-robbing disturbance of the thoughts that assaulted her with many confusions, she found release by wrapping herself in the bed's quilt coverlet, and was asleep in only a moment.

When she awoke, it was without the slightest idea what time of the day it was, or how long she had slept. She knew she felt more rested than she had for several days and was ravenously hungry. She found a water pitcher and basin on a washstand and freshened her face and combed her hair. She made short use of the enameled chamber pot, replaced its lid and placed it outside the door to her room. She locked the door behind herself and walked into the hotel's lobby.

The Seth Thomas clock on the wall above the desk clerk's head told her it was four o'clock. She had slept solidly for about six hours, and she felt better than she had in a very long while.

While making her way back to Fat Boy's Pool Hall, she stopped into a small bistro and treated herself to two soft cooked eggs, two rashers of bacon, a toasted roll with some quince jam, and a pot of black tea. Now totally her old self again, she felt she was ready to seek out Julio Esparza.

She walked slowly along the streets, making her way to the pool room. These were the same streets she had walked with a different purpose in mind not long ago. And while it had only been a couple of months since she had been here, it seemed to her to have been a lifetime away.

She had come to understand that before Daniel Ricardo had threatened her—before Antoine had offered to rescue her—and mostly before she had met Charlotte, she had walked these streets with no other purpose than to stay alive. There had been no future—no hope—and no end to cobblestone streets that went on and on forever and led nowhere except old age, rejection, and eventually death.

While it was true she had fostered the hope of someday being the madam of her own bordello, she now admitted to herself that she had always known in her heart it was an impossible dream. Now, however, the recent whirlwind of events that had taken place in her life had left her with a new and different perspective. The ownership of a brothel somehow sounded far more possible than it had not so long ago. Things had changed for her. There was the reality of hope for the future. If not a madam, then something else.

Since she had met Charlotte, she had come to feel there was more available to her than the dark future of the street walker. And then there was the strength and courage of Antoine. He had, by example, given her an air of confidence she had not known since those gentle days with her father.

As these thoughts were whirling through her mind, she noticed a young man dressed in the khaki slacks and shirt of a uniformed policeman. She hurried across the street in an effort to intersect his travel. It was obvious his destination was the pool hall. Halting directly in his path, she spoke to him through one of her finest smiles.

"Pardon me sir," she said politely.

In this neighborhood of Fat Boy's Pool Hall, Julio Esparza had quite often been approached by streetwalkers. Amber, though, dressed in the expensive and tasteful garb of Charlotte Romero, confused him. She certainly looked nothing like the women who had approached him before.

"Pardon me," she continued. "Are you the sheriff's deputy who is a friend to Claudia?"

"Claudia?" Julio managed.

"Claudia Van Fleet. Are you her friend?"

"You talkin' 'bout Claudia? I know Claudia. She's my best gal. Who are you?"

"I'm a good friend of hers. She found out I was comin' to Orleans, and she just begged me to see you."

"I ain't seen her in a month or so. Where is she?" Julio asked.

"Tennessee. Tennessee. She's in Tennessee," Amber lied.

"Why in the world would she be in Tennessee?"

"Well, that's where she's from, you know. Her Mama has taken real sick. You know what a good soul Claudia is. She's gone to care for her Mama. She said she really missed you though, and I should look for you near this pool room and tell you how much she misses you. She said she's gonna just be so glad to get back to you and prove just how much she loves you."

"She said all that?" Julio appeared thunder-struck.

"She said that and more. She said I should eat supper with you and find out all about what you've been doing. She told me the name of a place to eat that you liked, but I'm sorry, I forgot it. She said you and her ate there before."

"Must have meant the Fish House, I guess. We ate there once. Only time we ever ate together. Must be that what she's talkin' about."

"It surely must be. She gave me some money and said I was to pay for your supper."

"Damn! I reckon she really misses me!"

"Oh, you bet she does. Where is the Fish House? We should go there now. I'm all hungry as anything," Amber lied. After her recent meal she knew she'd need to be an actress.

"Over in the next square," he answered her.

"Well, let's go, Julie—she said she sometimes called you Julie. Let's just go and eat and share all the news about Claudia and you. Does the Fish House have wine? I'm just dying for a little glass of wine."

The Fish House turned out to be a very typical blue-collar establishment. It was the place that day workers stopped off for a shot and a beer to encourage them on the way to their labors. At sunset, as these same toilers made their way home, another shot and another beer soothed their drained bodies.

There were three tables with wire-backed chairs and checkered tablecloths centered in the room. Along the longest wall and across from the bar were three booths. Amber steered Julio into the rear booth, which she determined offered the most in privacy.

Once seated, they were immediately served by a large black woman. Her face was alight with a grand smile as she wiped her hands on the blue apron she wore. Amber knew she had recently sewn an identical garment.

"Bet ye'all love to have some fresh fiddlers," she offered. "Caught jest this mornin', they's just larrupin' good."

"Crabs?" Amber queried. "Fiddler crabs?"

"Oh no, Ma'am. These finest fiddler fish you can buy."

"Fiddlers here really good," Julio added. "I'm for fiddlers. Bring me a pair," he ordered.

"I suppose for me, too," Amber said, still not knowing what a fiddler was.

Fiddlers turned out to be smallish channel catfish, ten or eleven inches long, deep fried in a cauldron of oil flavored with hoarded leftover bacon drippings. A fist-sized portion of red beans and rice completed the meal. Amber had to agree with Julio that "fiddlers are really good". She made a great pretense of eating while actually hiding bits of fish and red beans within a denim napkin.

"Bring us some wine please," Amber requested.

"We got scuppernong. That do?"

Amber remembered having scuppernong wine with her father so very long ago. "Scuppernong be just fine," she replied.

Served in a water pitcher, she and Julio were soon on the third such container. Amber had been very careful to only sip modestly, but make an appearance of drinking quite as heartily as Julio. This was a skill most streetwalkers knew inherently. When Amber felt the deputy was drunk enough that she could ask a few pointed questions, she began.

"Claudia said there was one time she was really scared for you."

"When was that?"

"She said you found a dead man down on the docks. She told me she was afraid who killed him might get you, too. She said you're about the bravest man she ever knew. She said you weren't scared a bit."

"Brave, huh? She said that. Sometimes I thought Claudia just only liked me 'cause I was payin' her. Brave, she said I was brave? Well, I'm brave enough, I guess. Guess that body was pretty scary. Head all caved in and all. When's Claudia comin' back?"

"Soon—real soon. Did the constable find out who was the killer? Claudia said she bet that it was you."

"Well, this here Antoine, Antoine Acadia, took all his money out of the bank and caught himself a train and ran—got away clean, too. Then, don't you know he comes back just struttin' around town as big as you please. I said, 'Officer Homer sir'(Homer, he's the constable), I said, 'Look here, Homer. Here's that there killer'."

"Come back to town. Can you imagine the gall of that? We just grabbed him right up. Course my identifyin' him got him caught. Constable was mad at me for a month or so 'cause I didn't stop them Creole boys. Shoot, I knowed they didn't have no part in killin' that feller. Hells bells, they's the ones told me 'bout the dead man in the first place. They was the first to see him. Now, I ask you, if they killed him, how come they'd come and tell me 'bout him?"

"Creole boys? Did you tell Claudia about them?"

"I don't know, maybe I did. Anyway, constable's madder'n hell on account of I didn't grab 'em. I knowed they didn't do it."

"So, they just walked away?" Amber asked.

"Oh, I figured old Homer's gonna make me bring 'em in, so I did a little checkin'. I know who they are. Course it don't matter now."

"I'm interested," Amber said. "Sure, it don't matter, but I'd like to know. Who are they? Just curious."

"Bodoin brothers, Aldo and Mateo. Got a pretty sister. Magdelena, her name is. They's swampers. Lives back in Gator Hole."

"I've never heard of Gator Hole. Where in the world is that?"

"West of town—not too far. Pretty much back in the marsh though. Deep swamp out there."

"I'd like to see a place called Gator Hole. That sounds exciting. Would you take me sometime?"

"I ain't goin' back in there—just the meanest, trashiest folks we have lives in Gator Hole. You go back there dressed like you are, them rednecks have you peeled in about a minute."

"Are you just saying you don't know how to get there?"

"Bullshit! I know exactly how to get there. 'Scuse my language. I'm sorry."

"It's okay. I just want to know if you really know how to get to this place. Is there really a place called Gator Hole anyhow?"

"Have you ever been down on our docks— shrimper's place?"

"I might know where that is," Amber lied.

"Just on the west end of the docks is Oyster Path."

"Oyster Path?" Amber queried.

"Yep. It's a path—kind of wide—easy to find. Made up of some gravel but mostly oyster shell. You go along that path headed west. No trees. Not a shrub. Real open it is. You go 'bout a half a mile and now they's trees—big live oaks. 'Bout a thousand acres of nothin' but live oak forest and Spanish moss. Along about another half mile them Bodoin brothers got 'em a tarpaper.

"Sister lives there, too. I reckon they fish some. Hire out on a shrimper when they can. They's Spanish Creole. Harder workin' than French Creole usually. Always talkin' about honor and such. But they's a poor lot. My boss, Homer, says they'll starve afore they'll steal. I ain't believin' that, you know. They scramble ever day just to live, I'd reckon.

"Even so, they's others in Gator Hole that ain't Creole at all. The only honor they got is who can steal the most. I'm pretty sure they wouldn't mind doin' a killin' neither. 'Sides, that whole place is full of snakes and wolves and catamount panthers. There's skeeters down there big enough to stand flat-footed and screw a turkey. Aw, dang, there goes my language ag'in."

Amber did all she could to stifle her laughter. She thought the joke was hilarious, but tried to appear unamused by the vulgarity. Julio stopped here and filled his tin cup with another serving of the warm, red scuppernong.

"Julio, I'll be right back," Amber announced. "All this wine, I'm just gonna have to see the privy.

When I come back, I'm gonna want to hear more about your job. It just sounds so dangerous. Claudia said you were strong and brave, too. I can see that. I'll be back in a minute. Drink some more wine."

Julio busied himself with the wine and failed to see Amber slip some paper money to their waitress. Amber slipped out the back door that led to the privy and, in an instant, she was gone and headed for the Princess Hotel. She had, at least, heard some of what she had come for.

Chapter Seventeen

Amber found herself walking down streets so very familiar, yet from a past life long, long ago. These were the byways that she had strolled along so often, however on this day they seemed cold, foreign and alien. Clouds had begun to form over head and the afternoon sky was heavily overcast.

It was as if an ominous and foreboding gloom had settled itself above and throughout the city. Amber felt herself a stranger in an even stranger place. Even the soaring spires of Saint Agnes towering above the neighborhood seemed unfamiliar and threatening.

She passed the sewing factory where she and Claudia and Yvonne had spent so many hours at hard labor. The front door of the ancient building bore a faded sign that said:

CLOSED: BUILDING AND CONTENTS
FOR SALE OR TO LET, AUCTION SOON

A few more steps, and she found the doorway she was seeking. When she realized she was about to encounter a friend within the next minutes, a feeling of comfort settled over her.

The sign above the doorway bore the legend, GREENBAUM'S CLOTHING AND HARDWARE, CANDY, NOTIONS. A smaller red and yellow sign affixed to the glass window of the door read GUNS. As she entered the store, the top of the door activated a spring-mounted bell. It offered an adequate tinkling sound that immediately summoned the store's proprietor.

A thin, balding man in his sixties came towards Amber from the rear of a counter that bore rolls of fence wire and iron fence stakes. He wore a white shirt, topped with a celluloid collar, with a black leather bow tie and a dark blue pinstripe vest. He was busily wiping his glasses as he came forth to meet his customer.

"May I help you?" he said in a clear voice that had, in its day, greeted thousands of patrons.

"Uncle Israel, it's me," Amber responded. Replacing his spectacles, he peered through the gloom of the ancient storeroom.

"Oy vey! Is it you, Amber? Is it really you?"

"Truly me," she said. "Is it alright that I'm here in your store?"

"And just why would it not be good for you to be here?" He hurried to her and stood in front of her now, the two nearly touching.

"Well, I just thought some of your customers might not like to see me here."

"Pshaw!" he responded. "I like you more than my customers. Well, some of them anyhow. I'm so sorry I have not called on you for so long of a time."

"Well, actually, Uncle Israel, I've been out of town."

"Well, I'm glad you're here." His face dropped. "But I am sad to tell you I can't call on you anymore."

"And why would that be?" Amber wanted to know.

"Oh, I don't mean we can't be friends. I will always care for you, Amber. I just mean we can't see each other that way anymore."

"Tell me why," Amber queried.

"Well, you see, Amber, I've met someone. I'm gonna get married!"

"Really, Israel! Well I think that's truly fine." Amber was genuinely pleased. "Of course, I'll miss you as a regular. I had the most fun with you ever. But I'm glad you've found someone. You were so lonely. Tell me about her. I want to know all about her."

"Lonely?" he said, dreamily. "Yes. Golda passed on so long ago—long time." Suddenly his spirit soared. "Oh! Real fine Jew woman, I have now. Hilda, Hilda Lebowitz—German lady. She come from Hamburg with her husband Abram two years ago. Abram, he took sick and died. No one knows why. He just die. Leave Hilda—Hilda had no one. German, you know. She started cleaning shops here on the street to earn something. She cleans my store twice every week. I see her. I can't stop watching her. Oh, Amber, she's so pretty. Strong—helps me unload cartage. Makes corned beef and gefilte fish— so see, Amber, I have a woman now. We'll be married near Passover. So, I'm sorry, but I can't see you more. I'll never forget you, though. You were so kind—so sweet. When you need something, come see Uncle Israel. I always help you if you need. Not while Hilda is near, you understand?"

"Of course, I understand completely. You were kind, too. You were always so generous with me."

"I loved giving some money to you. I would think for days after about what you would buy with it. Something that would be a joy to you." He paused. "But I just cannot be with you in that way again."

"I didn't come here to see you for that Israel— not today."

"What then?"

"I want to buy some clothes. I said *buy*. I have money. I want some men's trousers, a shirt, and a jacket in my size. Oh, I also want some shoes. The kind the railroaders wear, the high-top ones."

"Why, Amber? What would you need those for?"

"I'm going hunting," she answered, and offered nothing more. As Israel gathered up the requested clothing, Amber stood in back of the fence wire counter and removed her clothing down to the skin.

"Where are you going to do this hunting?" Israel asked.

"Place called Gator Hole," Amber replied.

Israel made a stern face. "Creoles down there. Some ain't so good. Gator Hole can be dangerous for women."

"I'll need a pistol too, Uncle. A friend said I should have a U. S. revolver. Thirty-two," she said.

"For Gator Hole hunting, it's a good gun since a woman only goes there to love a man or to kill one. That's three more dollars." Israel made his way to the gun counter. "I'll load it for you, and give you some extra loads free, though." He handed the small blue steel revolver over to Amber.

It was a very inexpensive, but effective little breakdown pistol favored by storekeepers and bartenders. Often, it was referred to by its popular name, *Rainmaker*. She examined it carefully and tucked it into the pocket of the new jacket.

"I guess I'll need a union suit, too. Need some underwear, I think. Give me a red one—red flannel." Israel made quite a show of turning his vision away from Amber's nudity.

"Good gracious, Uncle, don't be so shy. You've seen me undressed many times."

"Ja, but then I wasn't getting myself married!"

In short order, Amber was clothed anew and ready for her foray into Gator Hole. She tried a hunter's cap on, but decided she could do without it. She paid her former lover for the clothing and placed her discarded clothes into a brown paper bag.

"Amber," Israel said in a pleading tone, "you might have some Gator Hole man scare you—you think you might be hurt—if you are afraid you point that gun right at his face and pull the trigger as many times as you can. Do you hear? Do you hear me?" he said earnestly.

"I do hear you, Uncle. I'm so glad you care about me, but I'll be alright." Before she left, she took Israel by the hand and drew him to her. Standing on tiptoe, she leaned forward and kissed Israel Greenbaum hard on the lips.

"Damn, I'm gonna miss that, Uncle," she said.

He watched her leave through the entry and heard the little bell above the door give its distinctive tinkle.

"Oy vey! Me too," Israel sighed.

Chapter Eighteen

It was the first time Claudia had seen a four-horse team. She had certainly noticed Oney Ledbetter's recent hard labors. It would have been harder not to. For the last two weeks, the Percherons had been harnessed every day and hauled load after load of firewood to the rear of the mansion. The result was a stack of precut fire logs that formed a massive pile that was both at once, long and tall. The freight wagon looked different today, too.

"Side boards," she thought aloud, "there's side boards."

When she asked Oney how much larger he intended the stack of wood, he replied, "We need about sixty to sixty-five cords for winter. Most folks figure a hundred and twenty-eight square feet to a cord, but Maude tells me to use a hundred and thirty. She says the 'rithmetic is easier that way. Any way you figure it, it takes a lot of wood and takes a lot of work."

"Leastways, I don't have to cut it like some folks does. Can't cut no firewood when there ain't no trees. All this here wood comes from just about everywhere—Oklahoma, Arkansas, Missouri—railcars hauls it in, then me and this here team hauls it out."

"You have four horses today. Why's that?" Claudia wanted to know.

"Later today, we haulin' a load of coal. Two loads if it don't get dark on us. These here Percherons mighty powerful, mighty powerful, and that's the truth. Haulin' coal though? Takes a bit of doin', even for the four."

"Seems like enough work. Ain't you all tired out, Oney? Can't Randall Big Turtle help you some?"

"Randall got his flower beds to ready for winter. He's plenty busy his own self. Funny thing," Oney said. "Parts of Kansas—winter not much different than Kentucky. Out here on the plains though, winter—well, probably harder than anything you seen afore—lots of snow drifts, lots of wind. Yep, I'm tired out, but I'll keep goin'. This ain't my first winter on the prairie."

Oney Ledbetter found himself at a loss for the right words. He wanted to explain things that he knew inherently, to a young woman, who had no idea in the world what he was talking about.

"This business of yours, Miss Claudia—well, for the next three or maybe four months, it just ain't gonna amount to much. Winter's about ready to set in. Here on the plains, we are going to have two big jobs for quite a while—three, four months maybe—

keepin' warm and keepin' the animals alive—cattle and horses, too."

"The woodpile you made ought to do for us," Claudia allowed. "What about the horses and those cows on the high meadow?"

"You thinkin' we got ourselves a wood pile? We'll burn every stick of it—coal, too. Be all gone by April. Weather here in April can be deceitful, too. A late spring makes a long winter. I'm bringin' the cows out of the high meadow. It's too far up there to haul in hay. 'Specially when the snow gets deep. 'Sides, that little creek up there freezes near solid. Cows can't make it, but about five or six days 'thout a drink."

"Can't they lick the snow? Eat it?"

"Yes, miss, they surely could. Problem is, they won't. They'll stand in snow up to their bellies and perish for lack of a swallow. Lucky for us, Mister Chris understood all about that."

"He did?" Claudia asked.

"Built that fine windmill, he did. Big cattle tank 'ttached to it. Holds enough water and the mill keeps apumpin' right along. You been around that tank. Do you know how it works?"

"I—I'm not sure."

"Well, that's where Mister Chris really knew his stuff. The top of the water freezes. Freezes six, maybe seven inches, hard and that's for sure. The windmill pumps water from the ground into the bottom of that tank though. That's where Mister Chris really knew what he was doin'.

"Tank's so deep it never freezes solid. Got drains at the bottom. By the way, should you ever want to see a sight, just climb up the windmill ladder. You can see for miles and more miles. 'Course it's all just prairie, but it's a sight to see anyway. Seems everybody wants to climb that ladder and have a look.

"But gettin' back to the water, we can drain fresh water from under the ice into the drinkin' troughs every day. Got so much water, Miss Charlotte 'llowed some of the neighbors to water here. Built the big barns the right way, too. All our barns face south. Afternoon sun in winter moves to the southwest. Helps keep the doorways dry and not so much mud. Critters comin' in and out can make a loblolly of muck."

"Southwest? I thought the sun just sat in the west," Claudia remarked.

"Some folks think that. 'Tain't so, though. Summer sun rises in the northeast and sets in the northwest. Winter comes—it rises in the southeast and sets in the southwest. And that's a fact, Miss Claudia."

"You just shut the cows up in the barn then?" Claudia guessed.

"Miss Claudia, you wouldn't have no way of knowin'—but no. You can't do that. You leave the front and back door to the barn open—ventilatin'. Cattle can get in and out of the wind. Our prevailin' wind is from the west. A barn built south to north gives 'em a good wind break. True, we get a hard norther once in a while, but they only last a day or two. West wind blows all winter.

"Was you to pen up the cattle and close them doors—well, pretty soon their breath and body heat start to condense—fills the air with moisture. Cattle breathe that in, and right away you got a sick herd. Can't allow them to breathe their own breath. All they need is food, water, and a place to get out of the wind. We do that for 'em—they'll fare pretty well."

"Oney, what would we ever do without you?"

"Well, all I know is you won't have to, 'lessen Maudie shoots me or a tree done fall on me." Feeling good about himself and having shared his expertise of Kansas winters with a novice, Oney walked away, singing a little song to himself he had known most of his life:

> *I'll eat when I'm hungry*
> *and drink when I'm dry*
> *If a limb don't fall on me*
> *I'll live till I die.*

Claudia turned and strode into the kitchen where she made herself a cup of strong black tea and watched Maude Ledbetter roll out a large sheet of dough. She then began to cut it in identical, small pieces for the creation of her perfect chicken and dumplings.

A large, fat hen was already simmering in an enameled pot amid a host of delicious flavorings. The kitchen had a smell about it that was a reminder of home, family, and all things good. Claudia glanced out the window and was surprised when she saw two women.

"Look, Maude. We got company."

Maude joined Claudia at the window. What she saw was two young women, each bearing a bulging suitcase, making their way up the long front lane to the house. When they approached the front of the house they disappeared from view. Both Maude and Claudia expected they would soon hear the front door chime or a sturdy rap. They waited, but no sound came for a long while.

Suddenly, they were startled by a rap at the kitchen door. The two women had skirted around the house and shown up at the back door. Maude was immediately suspicious of strange, young women showing up at Twin Oaks, since the appearance of Claudia and Yvonne left little doubt as to what they were there for.

"Answer it," commanded Maude. Claudia made her way to the door, teacup still in hand, and found herself staring at two young and pretty women.

"Whatcha' want?" Claudia greeted them. Looking them over, Claudia saw that she was addressing a tall, thin, redhaired girl with a lovely face, and a smile that beamed around exquisite straight white teeth. Standing next to her was a somewhat shorter, raven haired beauty with olive skin and a pouty mouth. She gazed up at Claudia with dark, mysterious eyes.

"We'd like to see the lady, Miss Amber. Are you Miss Amber?" It was the red-haired girl who seemed to be the spokesman.

"Naw, I'm not Amber. You could tell me what you want her for, though. I might be of help." Claudia had already sized up the pair. These were ponies. She'd know her kind anywhere.

"We were working down at Julian's—down the road. We were waitresses, at Julian's, you know. Well Julian—he left. So, we heard 'bout Miss Amber, and well, we wondered—could there be some work here for us?"

Maude felt her face flush crimson as Claudia invited them in. Maude Ledbetter understood the direction Twin Oaks was going for some time now. It was not a path she was for at all. Still, she and Oney had a good life here. She vowed she would

175

cook the meals, keep the kitchen, and otherwise be as absent as was possible. She started looking about for something to feed this pair of nomads as she knew what was coming next.

"I'm Briana." the tall one said. "Briana O'Flynn. This here's Rose. She ain't got no last name. Just Rose." Claudia accurately assessed that if Rose did have a last name it would certainly be very Spanish.

As for Briana O'Flynn, the lands of Ireland had sent more than a million souls into various ports of exile around the world since the famine of 1845 through 1851. A blight had swept through Ireland wiping out potato crops completely. When Britain's Prime Minister, Robert Peel, ordered all of Ireland's hogs, cattle and corn confiscated and moved to Mother England to feed the British army, famine replaced hope.

For years, Peel's critics would maintain it was his way of punishing a people who failed to give him the reverence he thought due him. The bountiful land was gone and would be blighted for decades. The million who left their native soil were the lucky ones. Another million starved and died, and the hate the people of Erin felt for the English would take root. Too young, perhaps, to be a refugee herself, Briana was likely the child of one.

Claudia went on, "Amber ain't here. But I know she'd want to talk with you, though. Gonna be a week—maybe a little longer. Can you come back sometime?"

"We ain't got no place to go, ma'am." Briana seemed pitiful. "Marshall Cole nailed doors shut at Julian's. There was a killin' there. Might be you heard? There ain't no Julian's anymore. Anyway, me'n Rose, we on hard times."

"Let me ask you, Briana—you and Rose—you got some steady customers? Men who would come to see you here?" Claudia was calculating.

"Got plenty to do, just no place to do it," was Briana's reply.

"We got to think this out. We got a chance here to get things goin'. Yvonne and me been sitting around 'bout long enough. Be good to make some money again." Claudia was becoming more and more excited as she assessed the opportunity that had just dropped into her lap.

"I know for sure Amber wants to be a madam more than anything. Maybe when she gets back home, she already is one."

Chapter Nineteen

Saint Anne's Parish Constable, Homer Chastain, was becoming angrier by the moment.

"Now, let me get this straight—you jackass! You sent a young, pretty woman alone to Gator Hole?"

"I didn't sent her nowhere." Julio Esparza was in physical pain from the neck up, as a result of far too much wine.

"She was askin' about them Creole brothers. I was just tellin' her they's whereabouts." Julio was deeply regretting he had ever mentioned last night's rendezvous with the pretty, mysterious stranger. He had only intended to explain his colossal hangover and, perhaps, to boast a bit about having fiddlers with a beautiful young woman. Due to skillful questioning by his superior, the whole of the evening's events had come to light. He realized now he had said too much.

He recalled that he was puzzled about the length of time she was visiting the privy, but after emptying the last pail of scuppernong, he simply forgot all about her. In fact, the next thing he remembered was the woman who had been their waitress shaking him awake and telling him it was time to close and that he should run along home. Now, he was deploring the fact that he had elected to tell the constable about it at all.

"Did you ask her how she even knew about those brothers? How did *you* know they were brothers?"

"Well, no. I thought Claudia told her. I just checked around a little. I found out they was brothers." Julio was beginning to squirm. It seemed that since he had come to the constable with the report of the dead body of Daniel Ricardo being found in the dock area, he had seldom done anything that Homer was in agreement with.

"But I never sent no woman to Gator Hole—I'd never do anything dumb as that!"

"Did she ask you to take her?"

"She did. And, I told her no!" Julio was firm in making his point.

"Did she then ask you how to get there?"

"Well, yes—I guess she did."

"You told her about the oyster path?"

"Well, I guess I did. But I told her it was a real bad place."

"You refused to take her, but you told her how to get there? You *sent* her, you stupid horse turd!" Constable Chastain turned on his heel. From the wall rack, he selected a Winchester rifle. He levered a live round into the chamber and turned to his deputy.

"What did you tell her about this prisoner? Antoine Acadia?"

"Just that we had him. That he left town with about ninety thousand dollars, but he was so stupid he came back and I—you nabbed his ass."

"Did you wonder why she was so full of questions about him? About the Creole brothers?"

"She said she was just curious. She said my old girlfriend Claudia—well, Claudia told her all about it."

"Claudia, my ass! You just opened your mouth, poured wine in, and everything else fell out. You just got your brains picked clean."

"I don't understand—what difference does it make?"

"She's *with* him, you dumb shit! Can't you see anything till it runs over you. She's lookin' for something to tell a lawyer."

"Lawyer?"

"Yeah—lawyer. Do you think we could hold this Antoine fellow if a lawyer knew two Creole boys— brothers it turns out, were the ones told a deputy they found the body? Get my buggy, Julio. Be quick about it. If anybody asks for me, I'm goin' to Gator Hole."

"I'm gonna see if there's anything left of your wine drinkin' buddy. That bunch of ne'er-do-wells down in that swamp probably fed her to the bobcats by now. When I bring her back in here, you keep the hell away from her. I don't want her findin' out from you whether I been circumcised or not."

"Aw hell, Homer," Julio stammered, "how would I know anything about that?"

"Just shut up, Julio, just shut the hell up!"

–oOo–

The November afternoon was warm and sunny, and the warmth of the sun felt pleasant on Amber's face as she walked along the gravel and oyster shell path. Skirting the pleasant little beach at the gulf's edge, she thought of Kansas and wondered if the day was as pleasant there. She decided it was probably not. The small waves lapping the shore provided a gentle cadence for her hike.

As she hiked along, she felt good in her new clothes. The new khaki pants were a little stiff and the jacket cut a little too straight for Amber's womanly figure, but, all in all, they were the exact garments one would select for such an outdoor adventure. Surprisingly, the heavy, railroader shoes were the most comfortable of all. Wearing the brogans over a soft cushiony sock were perfect footwear for the gravel and oyster shell trail.

Unfortunately, the pleasant path along the beach vanished all too soon. Looking up ahead, she became aware that she would soon be entering a brackish swamp, bordered on the north edge by a wide creek that originated somewhere miles away from the waters of the Mississippi, and on its south edge by the Gulf of Mexico.

This was a natural estuary perfect for all flora and fauna associated with bayou and marshland life. It was hardly a fit place for human life, and yet, Gator Hole held a community of its own people who would never leave even if an opportunity were offered.

This place was confusing to the senses. From the south came the fresh smell of the great body of saltwater, but that was comingled with the swamp smells of decay and stale water that had laid dormant far too long.

At the outer edge of the marsh, a few stately cypresses with their misshapen trunks seemed to mark the way into a far darker land covered in live oak and sinister drapes of Spanish moss.

Amber had barely entered this area when it seemed to her the sun had been turned off. As the gloom settled upon her, the oyster path disappeared and became a trail of hard packed earth, that she assumed would be impassible after a hard, soaking rain.

She saw a peculiar assortment of structures tucked back into the trees. They were disheveled forms of many varied shapes and sizes. Here was a log hut next to a canvas tent. Old lumber and corrugated metal of every sort and shape had been gathered from somewhere and everywhere and dragged back and assembled here to form some type of a rude shelter. Cooking fires smoked and filled the air with smells of ash and smoke.

It seemed to Amber there may have been twenty or more of these ramshackle huts which formed the community known as Gator Hole. She was searching for a particular shack, however: one made of tarpaper.

All about Amber, the bullfrogs groaned, sounding like cattle back in the marsh. Spring peepers filled the air with their trill. Amber treaded carefully, watching for the deadly cottonmouth that could be on the lane. As Julio had warned her, the mosquito population was aggressive.

Two towheaded youngsters, a boy of seven or eight and a girl of five, sat in the front of a squalid cabin tormenting a cat. As she walked past them, she was aware of a bald man with a beard, who was peeping at her from behind a tree trunk.

An old woman clad in a sailcloth dress scurried across the lane fifty yards ahead of her. The weight of the small pistol in the front pocket of the khaki trousers was a solid comfort as she drifted deeper and deeper into the hinterland.

All at once, it was there, a crude shack constructed of discarded canvas sails, salvaged tarpaper, and old wooden container sides.

An overstuffed, velvet-covered couch, gleaned from somewhere, sat in the cleared area directly in front of the shack door in a space that might have been called a yard. Two young men sat on wooden kitchen chairs smoking hand-rolled cigarettes. Eyeing Amber as she approached, they exchanged glances. Neither spoke or in any way acknowledged her approach. When Amber was within twenty feet of the pair, it was she who spoke first.

"Are you the Bodoin brothers? I'm lookin' for Mateo and Aldo." Amber examined the two as they watched her in stony silence. They were alike in size. Dark of complexion with raven hair, they were thin and crudely clad in the canvas pants and vest typical of the area shrimpers. Amber thought in another place and time they might have been called attractive.

"I'm looking for the Bodoin boys. Could you be them?"

After another lengthy pause, one of the pair left his chair and, in silence, began to advance toward Amber. When he was within reaching distance, he extended his arm toward her shoulder. Amber was more than a little experienced with men attempting to grab her. She inherently knew hesitation would lead to a more serious situation.

She swiftly dropped her shoulder and stepped in closer toward the man accosting her. With one direct move, she kicked out as hard as she could and connected the toe of the heavy work shoe directly with the shin of Aldo Bodoin. He cried out against the excruciating pain, and grabbing his injured shin, collapsed to the ground. Amber's second kick was even more devastating. Aiming the kick for his head, the heavy-soled shoe caught him just under the nose and squarely on the upper lip. He moaned heavily and rolled over on his side.

Looking up, Amber saw his brother leap from his chair and start toward her. It only took a second, and Amber had retrieved her pistol from her pocket and was pointing it squarely at the face of Mateo Bodoin. Seeing he was facing a gun, he froze in his tracks.

"I was not coming at you," he stammered. "I was coming to help my brother."

Amber took two steps back and allowed Mateo to kneel beside his brother. He tried to comfort him, and with an old bandanna he wiped the blood away from Aldo's broken face.

"You didn't have to hurt him so. He was not going to hurt you. He was only playing."

"Me, too," said Amber. She was becoming aware that covert eyes were watching this incident. She spotted one man behind a nearby tree, and another peering at her from a crevice in the wall of an adjacent shack. From a crack in the canvas front door of the tarpaper, she saw the pretty face of a young girl.

That's Magdalena, she thought.

"What do you want here? Why have you come to Gator Hole dressed like a man? Who are you, and what is it you want?" Mateo was keeping his eye on the pistol.

"I wanted to see two Spanish Creole men, who have no honor," she said. "Two cowards who do murder, then run away and hide. Two weaklings who allow another—an innocent man—to be blamed for their perfidy, and have no courage to come forth and claim their due."

"I don't know what you say." Aldo was trying to speak and staunch the flow of blood from his nose and mouth at the same time.

"Liar!" Amber barked. "Coward and a liar, too. You were the killers of Daniel Ricardo. Embarrassments to the proud race of Spanish Creole. Scum in the eyes of men who put honor before life. So vile, no good woman would care to whelp your offspring. My only question is: how would weaklings like you ever crush a man's skull? What weapon did you strike him with? Surely not your fist."

"*Martillo*," said Aldo.

"*Martillo*? What's that?" Amber wanted to know.

"*Martillo*, you say—*hammer*." He withdrew from his pocket a round piece of lead about four inches long and as large around as a half dollar. He closed his fist around the lead bar and struck his open palm.

"Hammer," he repeated, "*Martillo*. This man Ricardo—no, this dog, he takes Magdalena—wants to sell her love to men for money. Mateo hold him, I strike him with *martillo*."

"I knew it. I knew you killed him." Amber looked up in time to see the girl from inside the shack coming toward them. She was holding a single-barreled shotgun.

"It does not matter what you know," Magdalena said. "You'll never leave Gator Hole." She started to raise the gun. The startling blast from behind Amber was deafening among the closeness of the surrounding forest. Amber thought she had been shot and immediately looked down at her breast, checking for the wound.

"Everybody jus' stand real still," a man's stern voice commanded. "Drop that shotgun, sister...Do it now!" Magdalena complied. "And you, missy, with that lady's popgun—drop it. Do it now!"

Amber dropped the pistol to the ground and turned around to face the voice. Without ever seeing him before, she knew in an instant she was looking at the face of Julio Esparza's boss, Constable Homer Chastain. The explosion came from his rifle that he had fired into the air.

The next happenings came about so fast, they were a blur to Amber. The practiced lawman that he was, in only an instant, Homer claimed the shotgun, unloaded it and threw it as far as he could out into the waters of the swamp. He gathered the two brothers and Amber at his side and handcuffed the brothers together.

"That's all the cuffs I have, little miss. But if you get any ideas about runnin' on me or giv'n me any trouble at all, well, it's enough for you to know that I'll do whatever I have to."

"Listen to me!" the constable loudly shouted. "I'm takin' these three people along with me. I got a good Winchester rifle with me, and if any of you redneck peckerwoods try to interfere with me, I'll shoot you deader than cordwood. We're leaving now, and I better not see a single one of you frog-giggers in my way." As he turned his back to Amber for an instant, she snatched her pistol from the grass and buried it in a front trouser pocket.

The trip back into town was excruciatingly slow. Amber sat beside the constable on the seat of the Studebaker, while the brothers walked behind and were handcuffed to the rear of the buggy. Chastain had to hold the horse to the very slowest walk, in order not to drag the Bodoins.

"You heard them admit to killin' Daniel Ricardo?" Amber asked.

"That I did," Homer replied.

"Well, when we get back into town, can you let Antoine Acadia go now?"

"Not very likely, sister. Oh, I'm going to jail this pair for sure. But we got a lot more to find out about Mister Acadia. I'm pretty sure he's guilty of something. I just need to find out what it is. Oh, and I got some plans for you, too. I'm dropping you at the depot. New Orleans ain't no safe place for you anymore. I want you on a train out of town tonight."

"What about the hotel? I got stuff there. Can't I go to the hotel?"

"Did you hear what I said? I want you out of here. Now. Tonight. I saw you fetch your pistol, and I'm gonna let you keep it. Them cottonmouths from the Hole ain't likely to be happy with you bringin' a constable down there. One of them might decide to come for you. I almost wish they'd get you—all the trouble you caused me."

"Trouble? What trouble? I helped you get these two." She tossed her head in the direction of the manacled Bodoins.

"Let's just say the prosecutor's office and my bosses and all the voters in Saint Anne's Parish are likely to take a dim view of me arresting an innocent man. Then to have my irresponsible deputy send a slip of a girl like you to collar these here guilty brothers—and in a place like Gator Hole, for Christ's sake. Let's just say I ain't expecting a lot of back-patting for makin' this arrest—damn it, you little trollop! You're just more trouble than you're worth. I want you gone—tonight!"

"You just want me gone so nobody ever hears the whole story, right?"

"Don't make me change my mind. I got jail cells that ain't nobody seen in fifty years. You could just disappear, you know?"

"What if there ain't no train to Kansas tonight?"

"By God, you stay in that depot until there is a train!"

"But don't I need to be a witness or something?" Amber was distressed and frustrated at the way this was turning out. She was also glad she had worn her money belt, when she had, at one point, thought it might be safer in the hotel than in Gator Hole.

"It would come out in a minute if you were called as a witness. Everyone would know what you were—what you have been. Hell, I figured it out in a minute after we met. Your testimony in a trial would hurt Acadia lot more than help him. Whore's testimony ain't gonna never do nobody no good."

Homer Chastain's words stung like a bullwhip's lash. He had accomplished what no one before him ever had. She tried, to no avail, to stop the tears leaking from her eyes. For the first time in her life, Amber felt ashamed.

Chapter Twenty

Amber stepped down from the train at the now familiar depot just at sunrise. The November morning was quite chilly, but at least the wind was still. She drew Charlotte's shawl up about her shoulders a bit higher and began to look about for some transportation to Twin Oaks.

It was less than quarter of an hour later when her old acquaintance, Charles, came around the corner at the helm of his two-seat buggy and his nice brace of blacks.

"Missy—Miss Amber. It's me, Charles! I seed you step off that train, and I says to these two old soldiers, 'That's Miss Amber from out there at Twin Oaks.' I almost didn't know you. You bein' dressed like that. Doin' a little possum huntin', was you? I says to this here team, 'We needs to see her to home.' I hurries 'em up into the harness so's we can pick you up afore you gets too tired. Being on that train and all." In only a moment, he had seated Amber in the rear seat and provided her with a soft, woolen lap robe.

"Dear Charles." Amber had hardly ever been so happy to see someone. "I'm so glad you're here. I'm so glad to see Punch and Judy again." She nestled deeper in her shawl, and Charles realized she was chilled.

"Miss Amber, maybe it ain't right for me to ask you this, but would you care to have a little sip of 'shine? I makes it my own self and so I know it's right good. Take this mornin' chill right away."

"You know, Charles, that's just what I need. I'd welcome a taste of your 'shine."

Charles made a great deal of wiping the neck of the flat pint bottle and offered it to Amber. She took a tiny sip at first, not knowing quite what to expect. She had heard stories of mountain dew so fiery one might strangle on it. Instead, what she tasted was a smooth, bourbon-like flavor with little heat and a taste of smoky, delectable homemade whiskey.

"Hot dang, Charles! That's good!" She tipped the flask and had another swallow. "Do you ever sell any of this?"

"I gets four dollars a gallon, but I only sells to friends ain't gonna tell where it comes from."

"Do you have some now? Say two gallons?" Amber wanted to know.

"Happens I got me two gallons right here in the back trunk." He gestured toward the storage compartment on the back of the buggy.

She was warmed by the pleasant double shot of Charles' 'shine. That, coupled with the exhaustion of the long train journey and the events of the last several days, Amber slept more soundly than she had for a very long time. She slept for the remainder of the ride with Charles and Punch and Judy to the land of Twin Oaks.

Her midmorning arrival was met with shrieks of welcome from Claudia and Yvonne. They scampered down the lane and met Amber at the buggy as Charles was helping her alight. Excited as they were to see her, it only took a moment for the subject of Antoine's absence to become the topic of choice. The questions came from Claudia in a flood.

"Did you see him? Are they gonna turn him loose? Did you locate Julio? What about the Creole brothers? Are you alright? Did they try to arrest you too? Did you know we open the house for guests every night? Are you alright with that? Wait till you see our two new ponies—er—hostesses. They're beautiful—smart, too. Worked at that place called Julian's."

"Whoa! Ease it up. I can't handle all this at one time. Help me get this stuff up to the house."

Charles handed each woman a gallon earthen jug filled to the neck with a clear liquid.

"This is moonshine," Yvonne said. "I know moonshine, but why moonshine?"

"Where's your suitcase?" Claudia wanted to know. "Why are you dressed like that? Have you been, hunting? Possum hunting?"

"Lost the suitcase. Charlotte's clothes, too. I need a bath and something clean pretty soon. Am I starting to smell yet? Let's just get to the house."

Amber was more than glad to be home in spite of the whirlwind of questions. She fished a coin from the money belt and handed it over to Charles, who made a colorful show of accounting and giving Amber back the unused portion of the gold ten spot.

"Jest eight dollars for the 'shine, Miss Amber. Ride's on me—me and old Punch and Judy." The carriage master resumed his seat at the driver's post and, with two clucks of his tongue, they were gone.

When the trio entered the front door, they were greeted by Maude Ledbetter, Briana O'Flynn, and the dark-eyed beauty, who was now called Mexican Rose.

Maude greeted Amber enthusiastically and hurried off to make some midday meals she called dinner for the five. After the expected niceties and hand clasping and buddy hugging, Briana sensed the three comrades needed alone time. She motioned for Mexican Rose, and the two of them said polite goodbyes and disappeared into the bowels of the mansion.

Amber told the entire story of the meeting with Julio Esparza, the trek into Gator Hole, and the climax involving Constable Chastain. It was the Gator Hole portion of her story that rendered Claudia and Yvonne speechless.

"Weren't you scared?" Yvonne wanted to know. "I would have been. Damn, you're lucky you're alright. Weren't you scared though?"

"I'll be alright soon's I change my drawers." That brought the day's first smiles. When the smiles were over, and Maude had fed all five a nice lunch of thick bacon slices, hard cooked eggs, and butterbeans, Claudia and Amber, along with Yvonne, retired to the living room.

Claudia took the lead and began to tell Amber of how, for the past three nights, the four girls had begun entertaining men each night.

"Took in more'n sixty dollars," she said. "I put it in one of Maude's jars in the kitchen. It's all there, Amber. I'd never cheat you."

"I know that, Claudia. Did the other girls—that Briana and Rose work alright?"

"I tell you, girls was all good. Men had a lot of fun. Spent some money, too. They was put out that we didn't have the bar open and the card tables was closed. We told 'em soon's you back we be wide open and rarin' to go. Oh, that Marshall, he was here."

"Yeah, here twice he was," Yvonne added

"You mean Grady? Grady was here?"

"Oh, now it's Grady, is it? What's goin' on here, Amber?"

"Nothing's goin' on. It just surprised me, that's all. Was everything alright with him?"

"Perfect," Claudia replied. "Said if we kept the rules he laid down, all was well. Said soon's you get back, he'll be out to see you. I'd bet he's gonna ask you for some of that money we took in."

"Yeah, no surprise there. He says not, but you know how things work." After a moment's thought, she turned to Yvonne.

"How are you, Vonnie?" Amber wanted to know. Yvonne lowered her head and did not speak. "What can I do to help you, Vonnie? I'll do anything for you. It breaks my heart to see you so melancholy."

"I'll tell you how she is," Claudia chimed in. "She's bluer than a bruise on a plum. That's how she is. I keep tellin' her things are gonna be alright. She just ain't havin' it."

Sensing the subject matter was becoming somewhat morose, the trio faded away into their respective rooms. At nine o'clock, Claudia put the red lantern on the porch.

Twin Oaks hosted another night of gaiety. Amber opened the card tables, and Yvonne poured

Charles' whiskey at the bar for twenty cents a shot. The drinkers smacked their lips in approval of the tasty ware. Amber was as happy as they, realizing the four-dollar gallon of 'shine would bring in more than twenty-five dollars.

Yvonne should have been happy, too, as every customer left her a generous gratuity. Instead, she pocketed the money and muttered a rather straight-faced thank you. The other girls more than made up for it with lots of laughter, teasing, and good-natured cajoling.

Aside from the gaming tables and the generous pouring of good whiskey, the bedrooms did a brisk business as well. Girls were passing each other in the hallways as they led their clients into the private areas of the mansion.

A common occurrence was for a visiting client to select Amber for his private entertainment. She would good-naturedly, but firmly, reject these advances and steer her paramour to one of the other hostesses. She had decided she was completely finished with that side of her business, and never abandoned her resolve. She embraced the role of Madam now and, although completely new to the role, she was good at it. She could not even explain her decision to follow this position to herself, but she knew it had something to do with Charlotte, and something to do with character.

Undetected, the success of Twin Oaks was about to, at least temporarily, end. The hostesses, being unfamiliar with prairie winters, had no clue about how much things were about to severely change.

As November approached, the house drew about itself a cloak of dejection. Each day grew progressively shorter, yet the darkness hours produced fewer and fewer clients. The poker tables were mostly deserted night after night, and no twenty cent shots of Charles' good whiskey were crossing the bar.

No clients were showing up for those moments of personal experience with a hostess as Antoine had described it. In fact, while the hostesses of Twin Oaks had very much enjoyed their new status assigned to them by Antoine, the women of Twin Oaks longed for an old-fashioned, rowdy, cat house atmosphere where a girl could make some money and have a little fun. Winter gales halted the enterprise to a near stop.

Especially morose was Yvonne. Her belly was starting to show her condition, and she constantly moped about the deserted halls and rooms of the mansion that were once so filled with laughter and excitement.

Amber was equally dispirited. No news of Antoine for all this time had her feeling frustrated and defeated.

One late afternoon in the living room, Amber found herself commiserating with Yvonne and Claudia. As they each bared their soul to one another, describing their feelings of dejection and sadness, it was Claudia who decided she had heard enough, and with her astounding sense of humor, took control of the gloomy atmosphere.

"Here's to our Vonnie," she chanted, "so melancholy. She's got a belly like a melon and a face like a collie."

At first the little song took Yvonne and Amber by surprise. Then they began to chuckle a bit. The chuckles soon gave way to honest laughter, and finally the three were overcome by hooting guffaws and side-splitting, uncontrollable howls. Their stomachs ached from laughing, and tears flowed from the eyes of the three, who were now given over to shrieks and hysterical amusement.

The trio collapsed in each other's arms onto the sofa, and the glee continued out of control until Sally Two Feather, waiting, listening outside the room as usual, could bear their foolishness no longer. The previous gloom of the room had given way to an overkill of mirth.

"Y'all stop bein' so damned silly. Quit all this horsin' around and heist your asses out of here. I got to clean this here room."

When the giggling and mirth finally subsided, Amber said, "Oney said it'd be like this. Not much business at all till the trail herds start up again. He told me the cattle buyers from Chicago and Saint Louis would likely be our first customers, but they don't reopen their offices till the middle of April. I guess we'll just have to hold on till then. You got any thoughts, Claudia?"

"I think we'd better learn how to play five-handed gin or come up with a couple more sewing machines."

Chapter Twenty-one

It was two days before Christmas and nearly eight o'clock in the morning when Sally Two Feather slipped into Amber's room.

"Miss Amber, you need to be waking up. There's a man coming this way up the road. Man walking on the road. I think it might be Mister Antoine."

It took a moment for Amber to wake herself enough to understand what Sally had said. Once she became alert enough, she sprang from her bed as if propelled by springs.

"Antoine!" she cried. Throwing on a robe, she bounded toward the door. "My slippers, Sally! Find my slippers!" Now in robe and slippers, she bounded down the stairs, out the front door, and went racing down the lane to meet Antoine at the road. When he was still fifty yards away, she recognized that it was, indeed, Antoine.

Clad in the same clothing she had last seen him wearing, but now he clutched a blanket around his head and about his shoulders. His weariness was evident as he slowly put one foot before the other.

He obviously had walked from the railroad station in the early morning cold.

Antoine spied her heading his way and they both accelerated to full speed and ran to meet each other. Falling into each other's arms, it was a reunion of mixed emotions. First, there were the joys of reunion. Then came the flood of tears that erased the fears that they might never see each other again. They clutched at each other as they navigated the path leading to the warmth of the house.

They would never be lovers, nor would they ever yearn to be. Yet a bond existed between them that was as strong and undeniable as any marriage vow ever spoken. After all, Antoine had volunteered to kill a man for Amber's protection. She had braved the dangers of Gator Hole seeking Antoine's freedom. Theirs was a love as deep as the bond of brothers and sisters.

"They finally cut you loose, and cleared the jailhouse," Claudia said.

"Not exactly," Antoine replied. "They escorted me to the depot on a flat wagon. Put me on a train that was already moving. Told me if I ever come back, they'd shoot me. I said, 'give me the money I had when you arrested me.' Constable said he used my money to buy me a railroad ticket. Took a little more than two hundred dollars to pay for a sixteen dollar ticket."

"Jailhouse arithmetic. It's a cheat," Claudia said

"That's right, Claudia. A cheat! You understand perfectly," Antoine offered. "You understand the thing better than I do."

"That's 'cuz I been in jail more than you," Claudia offered to a round of laughter.

Maude Ledbetter made her delightful chicken and dumplings along with a custard bread pudding for dessert. The meal was wonderful to Antoine who swore never to eat oatmeal porridge again. His reunion with Claudia and Yvonne, coupled with the introduction to Briana and Mexican Rose, just made the meeting that much more delightful.

The meal was served in the main dining room. An adjoining table was spread for Oney, Sally, Randall, and Maude. With very little smoke and no odor whatsoever, every lamp was aglow with expensive whale oil. Each burned brightly with very little smoke and no odor whatsoever.

It was Randall who remarked, "Been a while since the old girl's been lit up like this."

"Why would you walk all the way from the depot in the cold?" Amber asked the question of Antoine that had been troubling everyone. "Why didn't you have Charles bring you?"

"Our good pal Charles, I'm afraid, is in the Oceola city jail," Antoine said.

"Jail," Amber said, "whatever for?"

"Well, apparently Charles sold a little homemade whiskey when the jitney business was slow." The girls looked knowingly at each other.

"Why didn't the livery man bring you?"

"Said he would. Had to wait for his helper though. Couldn't leave the barn alone. Helper wasn't to show till nine. I just decided to hoof it. I was, well, let's say anxious to get here. Not a great decision. Colder than I thought."

"Where did you get that poor rag of a blanket you were wearing?" Maude wanted to know.

"Stole it from the barn. I think it's a horse blanket. Leastways it smells all horsey."

–oOo–

Four days after Antoine's return, he and Oney left in the very early morning for a trip into town. As Amber watched their departure, she thought it quite curious they rode horseback instead of using a carriage, as was their custom. It was nearly dark when they reappeared.

Antoine and Oney were settled in the rear seat behind Charles in his cabriolet carriage being drawn by his beloved blacks, Punch and Judy. The two

Twin Oaks' saddle mounts were tethered to the buggy's rear.

In short order, as if it was planned ahead, Charles moved into a warm, comfortable sleeping room in the back of the machine shed and blacksmith shop.

It was outfitted with a small coal stove, a table with two straight back chairs, a cot covered with a feather mattress, and a down comforter. A roughhewn, upright cabinet held a supply of cups, plates, eating utensils and a large water pitcher with matching basin. Punch and Judy joined the stable of horses in the main barn and, along with their teamster, became part of the permanent cadre of Twin Oaks.

After the joys of Antoine's return settled down, the dreariness of the Kansas winter resumed its pall over Twin Oaks.

Aside from the return of Antoine to Twin Oaks, the deep winter of Kansas provided little relief from boredom to the occupants. Truly, the decks of playing cards and the sewing machines were the daily respite from the cold and gloom. With no customers, the duties of the day were simply to keep the warming fires attended and serviced.

The deserted card tables and the empty bar brought about an unfamiliar and dismal shroud compared to what they had been before the winter had closed the trails. Even on the extraordinary sunny day, the relentless wind kept the occupants indoors.

It had become a game to see what entertaining or ridiculous article could be created at one of the treadle-powered stitchers. The women made a shawl from sewn-together lace doilies, a vest made from a gingham feed sack, brush pants stitched from sailcloth. As the hostesses of Twin Oaks experimented and played with the machines, their expertise began to approach artistry. Amber's machine, Mister Willcox Gibbs, had never been busier. About the only unusual happening important enough to be noticeable was the frequent appearance of the Federal Marshall, Grady Cole.

It was a usual state of affairs for Amber to venture from her upstairs bedroom at about eight or eight thirty in the morning. It had suddenly become a common occurrence for Grady Cole to be lounging in the kitchen sharing hot coffee with Maude Ledbetter. It seemed to Amber that Marshall Cole would make the five mile horseback ride from Oceola to Twin Oaks on any day the wind would lay a bit.

It seemed perfectly normal for Amber to plop herself down at the table and join them for morning coffee, and so she did. The conversation between the three mostly consisted of valueless chatter about the weather. They spoke of a longing for spring, the girls sewing machine creations, and Grady's new saddle. Sometimes Grady appeared two or even three times in a single week.

Antoine, a notoriously late sleeper, would occasionally awaken early enough to observe the morning coffee klatches between Amber and Grady. He and Grady would exchange greetings while eyeing each other suspiciously. Antoine never joined them, but often poured steaming coffee into his personal mug and made his way back to the privacy of his "Chamber" as he deemed to call his first-floor room. Both Grady and Antoine wondered what the other had planned for Amber's future.

Always at these coffee meetings, Maude would excuse herself, and after a bit begin her food preparation for the day, leaving Grady and Amber alone in their mundane discussions. Occasionally, Grady might linger till after nine or even nearly ten o'clock. Then he would say goodbye to Amber, mount his horse, and ride in the direction of town. He had once told Amber that if there was no snow, he could ride cross country and cut the journey nearly in half.

"Did you enjoy your coffee with the Marshall?" Maude asked one morning.

"Oh, I suppose so. He's nice. We just talked about Yvonne. You know, when the baby is coming.

I told him I thought June—maybe July. I don't know why, but he seemed interested." Amber was still not thoroughly convinced Grady was to be entirely trusted.

"You don't know *why*?" Maude asked. "You don't know *why* a man would horseback through the cold to come here and talk about the weather—about what the girls are sewing—about Yvonne's baby? Why a man would spend nearly a whole day in the saddle to have coffee here in my kitchen? I swear, Amber, you're about as smart as a hog." Maude Ledbetter strode from the kitchen in a huff. She left Amber in a state. Amber was not unaware. There was more to consider.

Constable Chastain's condemnation of her as they left Gator Hole had not left her. She would forever wonder if any man, any *good* man would truly want her as a companion—as a wife. Would her past always control her future? Indeed, was there such a man who could overlook, forgive, and forget her past lived out on the streets of New Orleans? She knew he would have to be remarkable, and the odds were thin, if he existed at all.

Chapter Twenty-two

Just when winter seemed to have decided to last forever, Oney came into the kitchen with a welcome announcement.

"I saw a robin, Maudy, eating the fruits off last season's prairie roses over by the cattle tank—just as big as you please."

"Bet he's a cold little fellow," Maude allowed. "But hey, it's April—time for robins—early birds. It's been so rainy and cold. You know, Oney, I think April's the saddest month of all."

"Yeah, gets your hopes up with a balmy day, and then comes a freezin' rain. No matter, though. A robin sure means it ain't gonna be as long as it has been."

"Can I help you with getting breakfasts ready, Maude?" It was Mexican Rose who had entered the kitchen to hear Oney tell about the robin.

"You can slice up some bacon, Rose. I got these biscuits ready for the oven if this old stove'll ever get hot enough. Fetch me a little more of that kindling. A little more kerosene, too. Just a dash."

The prediction made by Oney spurred by the robin's appearance was an accurate one. Spring opened up in a green explosion, flooding the prairie with her myriad of grasses, gaudy wildflowers, and the pungent odor of sage.

Along with the change in the weather came the cattle herds from Texas and Oklahoma, milling their way north and searching for the steel rails that would signal the end of their journey. Along with the herds, came the expected cattle buyers, bankers, cowboys, big money and the outlaws. As to be expected, more than a few of these would find their way to the entertainment so readily available within the elaborate mansion at Twin Oaks.

It was about the time Randall Big Turtle's tulips began to bloom that Antoine approached Amber with a question that he had struggled with for months.

"What does Yvonne plan to do with her baby after it's born?" he probed.

"What do you mean, Antoine? I's expect her to—well—raise her baby. I'm not sure I follow you."

"Well," Antoine stammered, "did she ever talk about giving up the baby—for adoption maybe?"

"Not to me. Really, I've never given it a thought. I just thought we'd all pitch in and help her with everything. Kind of like having a mascot, you know. Probably she would talk it over with Claudia before me. They're awfully close. Can I ask why you want to know?"

"Amber, do you remember—while we waited for that train that brought us here—I told you that some time you might be able to do something for me?"

"Sure, I recall that. You said we'd talk about it later."

"Well, now is later. Amber, I've always known that in a business like yours, sometimes a baby comes along unexpected—unexpected, and maybe even unwanted."

"True," Amber allowed. "It's one of the perils of this trade."

"A man like me may never have a child, you know. That doesn't keep me from wanting one. I could do a lot for a child. Far more than Yvonne would ever be able to."

"You, Antoine? Are you saying you'd like to have Yvonne's baby? You know, Antoine, it's not just a matter of money or the fact you're a man and she's an unmarried widow woman. It's *her* child— she's bound to love it—want it."

"Maybe not. You've seen how sad she is. Maybe—maybe she might see it different than you. I'm hoping she does not still think I killed that skunk, Daniel Ricardo. Anyway, could you find out for me? See if she'd give me the baby? I could give a child a fine life. Better than Yvonne. I could give her money."

"Antoine, you're bowling me over. I would never have guessed this, not in a million years. My first thought, though, is you should see Claudia. Of course, I'll help you in any way I can, but Claudia— Claudia knows Yvonne better than anybody. I don't think she still believes you had anything to do with Ricardo's death. She knows about the Creole brothers. Claudia told her all about that."

"Please, could you talk to Claudia for me, Amber? I don't know her as well as you. Get Claudia to feel her out about it. And this subject— well, this is a delicate thing. Amber, I need your help on this."

It was now that Amber saw how earnest, how desperate, her friend was. His eyes were pooling tears. She had never seen Antoine in this frame of mind.

"Of course, Antoine." She pulled him into her arms. "Of course, I will. I'll talk to Claudia— Yvonne, too, if I can." In her mind's eye she could see Antoine with a baby. What she saw was spectacular. Something wonderful for both Antoine and the tiny bundle nestled comfortably in his strong and gentle embrace. She knew in an instant Antoine would be wonderful father.

–oOo–

The warmth of spring weather brought along with it a flurry of activity to the cattle marketing area of Kansas. The Chicago and Saint Louis cattle buyers had opened their offices. Reports of approaching herds came daily, and the siding of railroad cattle cars lined the spur tracks for as far as one could see.

The staff of the buyer's offices had already learned the location of the poker tables, the friendly little bar, and the lovely ladies to be found at the residence some were beginning to call Amber's Place. The hostesses of Twin Oaks were already seeing the return of a lively commerce.

It was already late enough on a Friday evening that the girls were preparing themselves for another business evening at Twin Oaks when Antoine spied Grady striding his way. He instinctively knew what was about to ensue and had prepared himself for the inevitable.

For weeks on end, Antoine had become aware of Marshall Grady Cole's increased attention to Amber. Amber, herself, may have been fooled by Grady's coffee klatches with Maude Ledbetter, but Antoine was sure he saw a situation developing. The drinking of coffee, he knew, was a ruse Grady Cole was using to see Amber.

"Antoine, could you spare me a moment?" Grady asked.

"What is it, Marshall Cole? What can I do for you?"

"I hope you don't mind; I would like to ask you a question. Rather personal. Hope that's okay?" Grady was studying his boots.

"Ask away, Marshall."

"Well, what I wanted to know was—well, about you and Amber. I mean, I was interested in the nature of your friendship. Well, I meant, is it more than a friendship? I'm just asking."

"And tell me, Marshall Cole, just why would I discuss that with you?"

"Well, I was just trying to not step on anybody's toes."

"No! You were looking for a reason not to tell Amber what you want. How you feel. If I said to you that Amber and I were lovers, that would free you from ever speaking to her. It's what you're truly seeking. I know why—because you are a yellow coward. Afraid to go after the very one and the life you want so badly—afraid that if Amber were to respond to you, someone might say, 'Look! Marshall Grady's woman was once a pony!' You're scared. Scared you might be humiliated by some imbecile. You don't have enough courage to stand by her. Defend her. You don't deserve Amber. A coward like you is not entitled to the life and love she could give you."

"Listen, you big bastard! I don't have to take that kind of talk from you." Grady was insulted and furious.

"Of course, you have to take it. You have to take whatever from me I hand you. You know I could crush you with one hand. And if you were to pull that silly pistol, I'd make you eat it."

He was about to say more when, suddenly, Grady Cole's right fist caught him squarely on the point of his chin with such force it drove him backwards several steps. Dazed, Antoine struggled to regain his footing but at last his knees gave way and he crumpled to the floor.

"Get up!" Grady commanded. "On your feet, Mister Big Man. I've got a little more of this for you." Antoine moaned aloud and rubbed his chin as he sat on the floor.

"Up, you bastard! Get up and let's see how tough you are. How about it? Are you going to get up from there?"

"I think not," Antoine groaned.

Grady, seeing Antoine had had enough, spun on his boot heel and stalked out of the room.

"He'll go straight away to Amber now—just as he should," Antoine thought aloud. "All in all, that worked out pretty well," he grinned to himself.

It was two days later when Antoine walked out of the front door of Twin Oaks and discovered

Amber and Grady sitting side by side in the porch swing. Huddled together beneath a large woolen blanket, they were obviously embarrassed by Antoine's intrusion. Excusing himself for the interruption, Antoine turned on his heel and reentered the house, closing the front door behind him.

Amber and Grady shared an embarrassed giggle. Had Antoine only opened the door a moment sooner, he would have interrupted a long, impassioned kiss.

–oOo–

It was the third of July, 1872, when Yvonne gave birth. It was early morning when Sally Two Feather summoned Claudia to "Come now!" to Yvonne's room. "Baby come now, Claudia! You come."

With the ruckus raised by Sally, it was only a few moments until the entire residency of the Twin Oaks' house was out of their beds and standing in the hallway outside Yvonne's door.

"Betcha' it's a girl," Briana ventured.

"Can't be. She carried too low. Boy for sure!" said Maude Ledbetter.

"Don't talk so loud!" Amber was protective.

"Pray for Yvonne—pray for a good baby!" Antoine added.

Within the first half hour, the little band of waiters had grown silent. Now the first hour passed, and they sat on the carpeted floor. It was midway through the second hour that Claudia opened the bedroom door and stepped into the hallway. She was disheveled, and the blank look on her face and her slack jaw could have been confused with one in shock. It was, in fact, exhaustion. Finally, she managed to speak.

"It's a little boy," she announced, "a fine little boy. His name is the same as Yvonne's father. He is Woodrow."

Amber added, "Our little Woody."

Chapter Twenty-three

The rest of the summer of 1872 would not have been so notable had it not been for the diversion that was little Woodrow. The bordello continued to make money and provide entertainment for the exuberant cattle trade common to the area. The entire residency of Twin Oaks had assumed a status of shared parenthood. The main point of contention among the residents was whose turn it was to care for little Woody.

While every one of the Twin Oaks' denizens showered the little boy with care and affection, none was so obvious in his dedication as Antoine. He cuddled little Woody in his arms. He changed his napkins and gave him warm and soapy baths. Rocking him to sleep in the big rocker in the parlor was an everyday occurrence, with Antoine whisper-singing a strange, Spanish lullaby that no one had ever heard before.

The most memorable thing of the summer was the day Antoine hired a photographer to come to Twin Oaks to photograph Yvonne, little Woodrow and himself, in what was obviously a family portrait. Two weeks before, Antoine had asked Amber if she thought she might make him a suit.

"I'd like it to be three pieces," he said, "black with a vest."

Amber thought the request a bit unusual coming from Antoine, who never asked anyone for anything. However, she found a certain delight in doing something for him and showing off her sewing skills at the same time.

"It's beautiful," Antoine proclaimed, when Amber presented it to him. "Can I pay you something for it?"

"I used two yards of the good English wool. That's forty-eight cents each. Half a yard of silk for the lining—about a dime. You owe me a buck," she said, then added, "It's on the house." They each laughed as Antoine pressed a folded bill into her hand. She had given him facts he would remember.

The photographer, a funny little man in a checkered suit, came driving a miniature, covered wagon pulled by a singular, exhausted-looking mule. He arrived early one morning, and it would be nearly noon before he had fussily arranged his tripod, the rocking chair, and other variously assorted paraphernalia.

He seated Yvonne in the rocker. She wore the blue dress she had made and was her favorite. In positioning her, the photographer raised the hem of her skirt a few inches so that her high button shoes were evident. She looked almost angelic in the dress with an ivory-colored shirtwaist and little Woodrow cradled against her breast.

Antoine stood alongside of her with one hand on her shoulder and the other tucked into his suit jacket in a rather Napoleonic pose. At exactly the proper moment, baby Woodrow delighted the onlookers with a very appropriate, beaming smile, though the actual image created by the ten second exposure was a bit blurry.

After the glass photo plates had been processed, a collection of photos came less than a month later wrapped in a brown paper packet. Oney retrieved them from the Emporium General Store, which also served as Oceola's depot for Wells Fargo. The pictures were displayed throughout the house and were a delight for all that saw them. Amber was aware that Antoine was busily sending some of the photos to his family back in Spain. Indeed, she helped ready a few of the packets for mailing.

Why, she wondered, would he send out pictures of himself, a beautiful woman, and a charming baby without any accompanying letter of explanation? But then, she admitted to herself, she knew nothing of his family in Spain. He sent only pictures— nothing else.

No more was said about Amber finding whether or not Yvonne would consider giving up the baby for adoption. However, Antoine was often seen engaging in rather hushed conversations with Yvonne. They appeared to be communicating with each other very well, without the assistance of Amber or Claudia. It seemed a settled matter that little Woodrow and his mother were an integral part of the household and would remain so. It was to continue that way until the middle of October when the tranquility was upset.

"Amber, Amber," Antoine called from the living room. "Amber, I need you. Come here please." His voice was urgent.

Amber made her appearance from the hallway. "I'm here, Antoine. What's the matter?"

"Look at this," he said, handing her the pistol she had bought from Israel Greenbaum. "Where did this come from?"

Amber was astonished. "My lands!" she said, "I had forgotten that I even had that gun."

"It's your gun?" Antoine was amazed. "Why would you have a gun?"

"I bought it when I was in New Orleans. I thought I might need it when I went to Gator Hole."

"Gator Hole?" Antoine was incredulous. "When the hell were you ever in Gator Hole?"

"Antoine, tell me at once. Where did you get that gun?" she demanded. "Have you been searching my room?"

"Of course not. I took it from Vonnie. I found her sitting on the porch with this pistol in her lap."

"Oh, no," Amber was at once saddened and concerned. "What do you think about that? She must have found it in my dresser. I think that's where I put it. I forgot I even had it. Why would Yvonne have it?"

"I know what I think, Amber, and I don't like it at all. But when were you in Gator Hole? Why would you buy a gun?"

Amber thought long and hard. "I'd really not like to talk about that," she said.

"Not good enough, Amber. I know about Gator Hole. Some of the men I boxed with came from there. It's a dark and dangerous place. I want to know; why were you in Gator Hole? And with a gun, no less?"

"Why would Vonnie have my gun?" Amber asked, hoping to change the subject. "What would she want with a pistol?"

"You know the answer to that without even thinking about it."

"But she seemed so happy since the baby. I thought we were finished with all that sadness— melancholia. Didn't you think so?"

"I don't know what I thought. Sometimes she was all smiles. Then she'd just stare out a window for what seemed like hours. Who could tell what she was thinking? She's got a hurt someplace, Amber. Someplace down deep."

"What did she say when you took the gun?" Amber cut in quickly, still trying to avoid the subject of Gator Hole.

"She said she wanted to shoot a rat. Shoot a rat! Can you believe that? She handed me the gun and ran into the house. I think she was crying."

"Do you think we should try talking to her? Maybe try to cheer her up? What should we do, Antoine?"

"Enough! Stop avoiding my question, Amber. You know she was not going to shoot a rat! Tell me—what were you doing in a place like Gator Hole? Carrying a gun? When did this take place?" Antoine's voice was stern.

"When you were in jail. I learned about the brothers and thought I could help you get out of jail." Amber knew she was inviting a scolding.

"Brothers? You knew about Aldo and Mateo? Are you telling me you went searching for the Bodoins with a gun to get me out of jail?"

"Well, it worked, didn't it?"

"I thought it was Constable Chastain who rounded up the brothers," Antoine offered.

"Oh, horse shit!" Amber offered a rare bit of profanity. "He couldn't find his left foot. He ran me out of town before anyone could find out. I'm the one found the Creoles. He just found me."

Antoine collapsed onto the large sofa. Amber thought he looked pale and confused.

"I'm going to want to hear more of this story, Amber, the whole thing. How you went alone into Gator Hole with a gun, and rounded up two killers, and got me out of jail. Oh, you bet! I'm going to want to hear it all. But right now, I've just had all this day I can stand. I just am lost for words. I simply don't know what to say."

Amber, her courage up now, stood before him in a defiant mood. Feet apart, hands on her hips. "A thank you might work!"

–oOo–

The days of summer passed and, along with the fading sunlight, the customer count faded at Twin Oaks. Late fall and early winter brought a close to the cattle herds and, along with it, a lack of customers for the hostesses.

Oney was heard to say, "It can't last much longer. All the old wild longhorns have been gathered up by now. Every cow in Texas is wearin' a brand. No more wild cattle for free. 'Sides that, the railroaders are just buildin' spurs everywhere. Not much use in herdin' cows when you got a spur track crossin' your land."

The working girls of Twin Oaks paid little heed to this prophesy of doom, but Oney's wisdom in years to come was on target. Each passing year, the commerce of the house at the Oaks seemed to dwindle.

But for now, the girls were glad for the rest, and they decided to only worry about Oney's prediction when and if it really happened. It was now approaching Halloween and an ominous mood was creeping in. Mexican Rose spoke about the Day of the Dead, and Amber decided, just in case, to post lighted candles in the windows to honor restless spirits. Their efforts to appease uneasy spirits, however, fell short.

"Miss Amber! Miss Amber!" Randall Big Turtle's cries were frantic and constant. "Please, Miss Amber, come quickly!"

Hearing the frenzied cries, Amber ran to the backdoor and discovered Randall standing on the landing with the limp and drenched body of Yvonne in his arms. Horrified, she rushed forward to help him with his grisly burden.

"I found her in the cattle tank!" Randall exclaimed. "I climbed up the ladder to see how deep was the water, and when I looked over the side she was there, down 'bout three feet under and lookin' up right at me. Her eyes was open—I nearly fell. Scared me, I tell you. I never seen no dead person lookin' at me. Skinned my arm all up. I run to the shed and only could find me a hoe. Reached down in the water and hooked her with it. Tryin' to climb down the ladder with her—me and her fell most of the way down!"

Amber viewed her dear friend. The sad little Vonnie. Her face was ashen. Her lips a ghastly shade of blue. Her long, wet hair cascaded from the crook of Randall's arm. Saddest was her favorite blue dress, now soaked and dripping water on the kitchen landing.

"Oh, Vonnie, Vonnie," she cried. By now Maude and Claudia had gathered at Amber's side.

"She must have climbed the windmill ladder to look at the water—lookin' around, maybe. Seein' the view from the lookout. Slipped and fell in, I guess. Oh lord, it's just so, so terrible," Randall offered through his rasping breath.

"My sweet friend, my pal." Claudia was crying, sobbing so uncontrollably her words were almost indistinguishable.

"Bring her in, Randall." Maude was the only one left with a shred of control. "Take her to the parlor. Put her on the big sofa, Randall. Then you go fetch Oney. Get him up here quick."

"Antoine! Antoine!" Amber cried, "Come quick! Oh my God—Antoine, hurry, hurry here!"

Antoine came as soon as he heard Amber's shrill voice. He had heard Amber's voice long enough that he knew she was in a panic. He bolted through the house to be at her side. When he saw the pitiful burden in Randall's arms, he wasted not a moment. He quickly took Yvonne from Randall and headed for the parlor. Over his shoulder he shouted at Randall.

"Tell Oney, hitch a buggy. We got to get to a doctor! Go now!"

Maude placed her hand on Antoine's shoulder. "It ain't a doctor we're aneedin', Antoine. No doctor can help her now." Antoine immediately saw that Maude was right. In his panic and his concern for Amber and Claudia, he had failed to realize Yvonne was dead. From deep inside the house, he heard little Woodrow crying.

Chapter Twenty-four

As winter dragged on, the spirit of Twin Oaks languished. Yvonne's death the previous November was hard on everyone. At that time, Grady Cole and Oney had taken the flat wagon to Oceola and purchased a coffin. While in town, Grady paid a visit to Doctor Pritchard, who was also the coroner for the community.

"We got us an accidental drowning out to Twin Oaks, Doc. Girl named Yvonne Acadia. I think she climbed up on the windmill for a look-see and slipped into a big tank of water for the livestock. You want to see the body; I got her in a storage room in the back of the barn."

"One of them Twin Oaks' girls, was she? She got any kin around here?"

"She was a hostess, Reuben. Real nice lady. She has a husband and a little boy, too. The husband works on the place. They live right there, if you want to see him. Here's a picture they had made a little while ago." Grady pressed one of the recent photos into the doctor's hand.

"You've seen her, right? You feel good about it being an accident?" Doctor Pritchard wiped his glasses. "Nice family, I'd say," he reflected on the picture.

"Sure. Couldn't be nothing else. Just a pitiful accident. A real sad thing."

"You being okay with it, Grady, I don't have to see her. I'll get a death certificate for her husband in case there's any other heirs come showin' up. I'll get it in a day or so, and just put it in your box over to the post office. She goin' to the cemetery, or is she gonna be interred at home?"

"Home, I guess. Would you need anything else, Doc?"

"Reckon not. She got a little boy, you say? How old is he?"

"Just a baby, Doc. Few months old. Maybe four."

"It's sure too bad, ain't it? Just from climbin' up a windmill. Ain't it a shame?"

Grady stepped out of Doctor Pritchard's office and, at the end of the boardwalk, entered the *Oceola Weekly News* office.

"Look here at this picture, Tom."

Tom Prentiss, a thin man in his seventies, had published Oceola's only newspaper, the *Weekly News*, for more than fifty years.

"Nice lookin' family," he said. "News?"

"Yeah. Lady drowned. Fell into a cattle tank when there wasn't anybody around to help her out."

"Damn! That's sorrowful. This big fellow here—he's the husband?"

Grady spent a few minutes telling the editor the story of Mister and Missus Antoine Acadia and baby Woodrow. Most of it was concocted by Amber and Claudia.

"I'll write 'em up a nice obit, Grady. Can I keep the picture? I'll run it alongside. How about I put some copies in your mailbox?"

"Fine, Tom...that's just fine."

It was on the way back to Twin Oaks with the coffin on the bed of the flat wagon that Oney remarked, "I didn't know Yvonne and Antoine were married. Don't surprise me none. He sure looked after her and little Woody. I didn't know they was married...but you know, I sure am glad."

"I know, Oney—I sure am glad, too."

–oOo–

It was nearing Valentine's Day when Israel Greenbaum opened a strange package. It had been shipped to his store from someplace in Kansas.

"Who do I know in Kansas?" he wondered. "Who would send me something?" The packet was very well wrapped in several layers of brown paper, with an outer layer of oilcloth assuring a waterproof bundle. He unfolded the waxed, brown paper to reveal a fine, three-piece, black suit. A letter addressed to him lay atop the garment. For the moment, he ignored the letter and carefully unfolded and examined the coat, the vest and the trousers.

"Hilda! *Mein schatzi! Hilda, kommen sie hier!*" Hilda arrived to find her husband almost reverently examining a black suit.

"Look Hilda! What a wonderful garment. Look at these seams, the tightest I've ever seen. Do you know this fabric? Worsted wool! That's the finest. Feel it! See how hard the finish is? Keeps its creases. Springs back to life when it gets wrinkled. And this lining! Oy vey! Silk!"

"Who is sending you a suit, Israel? We have suits for sale. Why would someone send you a suit? We sell suits, do we not?"

"Not that many, and not like this. We sell suits for seven dollars. What do you think we could sell a suit like this for? How much?"

Hilda fingered the material. She examined the finely crafted seams. She trusted her husband's instinct for quality.

"I'm not sure, Izzy. It is so much nicer than our suits. Do you think we could sell it for..." she paused thinking. "Do I dare say fifteen dollars?"

"I'm thinkin' that too, Hilda. Fourteen ninety-five!"

Israel unfolded the letter and read it aloud to Hilda.

To Greenbaum General Store
520 West Street
New Orleans La.

Sir: *January 25, 1873*
I am a tailor. The suit you have received is a sample of my work. If you can sell garments such as this suit, I can provide them to you for eight dollars and seventy cents each. I can make suits for you in black, brown, and, if material is available, blue.

If this is of interest to you, write to A. Acadia. Twin Oaks Ranch. Oceola, Kansas. General Delivery.

Yours Truly,
Antoine Acadia

Chapter Twenty-five

In the years following the great Civil War, Kansas became known to some as the land of the outlaw. The most famous and notorious of this breed seemed to gravitate to the place others were calling the *sunflower state*. In many ways, the lands of Kansas were almost perfect for the desperado. The grassy plains stretched out so far, a man could lose himself within them for days on end. The far west end of the state shared the hills and rocky outcroppings of the neighboring Colorado territory, creating almost perfect hideaways and sanctuary for those with reason to avoid notoriety.

Mostly, though, the attractions of Kansas to the brigand were of the monetary type. Westbound travelers carried personal wealth to their destinations. Kansas boasted rich farmers, wealthy cattle producers, well-heeled miners. Further, there were countless saloons, brothels and gambling halls. These promised delights so alluring to a man on the run and, after long periods of the meanest existence, were irresistible.

Dodge City had its Longbranch, Wichita had the Oriental, and Oceola was famous for Twin Oaks.

These oases of pleasure were irresistible to hard working cowboys, miners, and planters. Along with them came the lawless. It seemed the most desperate of these either headquartered in the state of Kansas or at least passed through on a regular basis.

Frank and Jesse James knew Kansas well. As did the Youngers, the Doolins, and the Dalton brothers. One of these, not so famous but equally treacherous, was Al Jennings.

Well known as a lawyer turned train robber, it was a warm July evening when Jennings found his way to the card tables at Twin Oaks. Accompanied by a short heavy accomplice, both were dressed in bib overalls. They each donned striped, denim, peaked caps as disguises in an attempt to pass themselves as railroaders.

A few days before, the residents of the Oaks had celebrated the first birthday of little Woodrow Acadia, and a few paper lanterns and birthday candles still could be detected in the big room.

Jennings was so taken with his card playing, he failed to notice that the tall, thin man, who had just entered the room, was wearing a badge on his shirt that designated him as a United States Marshall.

From the daily study of countless wanted posters, Grady Cole recognized the outlaw Jennings instantly.

"Al Jennings! Throw up your hands! You too, fat man! Get 'em up. Right now," Grady commanded, drawing his revolver from his hip holster. "I'm warnin' you, right now. Either one of you goes for a gun, I'll shoot you both."

Jennings eyes shot around the room. It was crowded, and he figured that no lawman was likely to fire his gun into a room with so many people. At least, he hoped he would not.

He dived under the table and turned it upside down as he bolted for the side door. In a flash, he was running across the yard and heading for the tall horse he had tethered to the hitching rail. Jennings reached the road, vaulted to the saddle and his great horse ran wildly through the darkness with uninhibited abandon. Grady was about to give chase when the short, heavy man gained his attention. Jennings' accomplice was in no mood to run.

"I'll fight, you son of a bitch!" he barked, and retrieved a pistol secreted in a rear pocket and covered by the tail of his coat.

His pistol roared, and the noise from the short-barreled weapon, confined by the walls of the living room, was deafening. His shot, fired in such a hurried state of desperation, went wild and shattered the mirror above the fireplace. Grady took a moment to see that no one was in his line of fire behind the outlaw. He fired his forty-four Colt once, and the heavy bullet struck his assailant squarely in the chest. The bandit cried out in pain and slumped, dying, to the floor.

"Watch him, Antoine," Grady shouted and sprang for the door. Antoine was atop the dying man in an instant and snatched the revolver from his hand. Grady sprinted for the door and down the yard to his own horse.

The marshall and his mount were no match for the long-legged bay. Already with a minute's head start, the tall horse had no problem pulling even further away from Grady, and, within a minute or two, the outlaw's mount was so far ahead that Grady could no longer hear the hoof clatter.

Defeated, Grady returned to the living room at the Oaks. He was not surprised to see all the guests had fled. Only the residents were there, and they sat staring at each other completely unsettled. They each knew that they had been in the middle of a serious and deadly gunfight.

Antoine sat in the rocker holding little Woody in his arms. His face was ashen. The child's face was tear-streaked, because he been awakened from his slumber by the gunfire.

"Couldn't you catch him, Grady?" It was Amber who broke the stunned silence.

"No chance," Grady replied. "Racehorse. Jesse and Frank James started this thing of going to

Louisville, Kentucky, and buying racehorses. Now, a lot of other bandits and bad men are doing it, too. Nothing can catch them. They're wild and crazy. Not much good for anything else, but if you need a getaway, they fill the bill."

It was at that moment that Charles appeared in the doorway from the living room. He addressed Amber directly, "What's happenin' here, Miss Amber…You needin' some help. I heard some shootin'! Is that there a dead man on the floor?"

It was Grady who responded, "I know you—didn't I arrest you one time?"

"You did. You got me sellin' some 'shine. I don't do that no more. I'm just a stable-hand here for Miss Amber."

"Charles, ain't it? Your name is Charles?"

"Yes, sir. I sure am Charles."

"Let's pack this man out of here, Charles. We'll put him on the porch for now, then hook us up a wagon, and we'll take him to the coroner, Doc Pritchard. Grab his feet—let's go."

It was at that moment Antoine watched Charles and Grady struggle with moving the dead man, that he knew something had to be done to protect his son's safety.

Chapter Twenty-six

One thing that was truly accomplished by the visit of outlaw Al Jennings and his confederate, a man named Carl Everett, was the strengthening of Antoine's resolve to remove baby Woodrow from the environment of Twin Oaks. Everett turned out to be wanted in Oklahoma and Arkansas for horse theft.

From the beginning, Antoine had known a brothel was not a suitable surrounding for a child. Then, the possibility of more gunplay and an actual threat to the safety of the child had made his mind up to resolve this problem at once.

He called for Oney and instructed him to saddle two horses and to accompany him on a morning ride.

"I just have to tell you, Amber." Grady and Amber were having morning coffee in the kitchen. "I never would have figured that Woody was truly Antoine's son. Antoine told me that he and Yvonne were married months ago, but kept it secret. He swears the boy is his natural child. I tell you, Amber—I just find it hard to believe."

Amber carefully weighed her response. "Does it matter? The boy is safer and better cared for than he ever would have been in any other situation that *could* have been his future."

"Well, you're right. I'm just curious."

"Grady, last night you told me that you loved me. Did you really mean that?"

"Of course, I meant it."

"Then I would like to ask a favor of you. In the matter of Antoine, Vonnie, and Woody—just let it be."

"Of course, you're right, sweetheart—nothing to gain by even thinking about it. Right thing is let it be."

"Look, Grady." Amber was peering out the kitchen window. "There's Antoine and Oney on horseback. Where do think they're heading so early?" Amber queried. It was at this time Maude entered the kitchen.

"You folks alright for coffee?" she asked, cradling Woody against her breast.

"Coffee's fine, Maudy. Where's the horsemen headin' this morning"

"I sure wish I knew. They've had their heads together for more'n a week now. They cookin' up somethin', that's for sure. Told me this mornin' they may not be back till tomorrow. Somethin' strange goin' on, I think. Oney just ain't like that. Tells me everything, he does. Worrisome—just worrisome."

Chapter Twenty-seven

Antoine and Oney had been riding for more than four hours when Antoine called for a halt. The two dismounted and stood talking in the road next to a sign that read Haverford Six Miles.

"Tell me, Oney. Have you ever thought of you and Maudie having a place of your own?"

"Guess we wore out that idea long time ago, Antoine. We had a dream about that, and it was about to happen back in Kentucky. Jase Cox—you remember? Got in that trouble fightin' with him, I told you about, and we just run out of everything. Even dreams. Probably, things would have got even worse than they were if not for Mister Christof." Oney studied his boots intensely.

"Well, Jase Cox is a long way off. He's no problem now. What if I knew a way you could have the place you dreamed of? I know it's been a long time since you quit on that. Do you think you might get that dream going again?"

"Would I need to kill somebody?" Oney responded with a wry smile.

"Not take a life, Oney—save one."

"I'd sure be glad to listen, Mister Antoine."

"You might recall Haverford?" He gestured to the sign. "The little town where you and I found that bar we now have in the great room. Where we pour the whiskey?"

"Sure enough. I recall."

"Man named Oliver tryin' to sell a place over there. He comes to Twin Oaks sometimes. He never hangs out with the girls. Just cards and a little whiskey. Says he's got just under two hundred acres. He says there's a decent house and two barns. He claims it's on a big creek. Runs deep and clear even in August and September, he says. He says twenty-five hundred dollars takes it all."

"That's interesting—for someone. Maudie and me we're a long way from havin' that money."

"I'll buy it for you."

"What!? What are you sayin', Antoine?"

"I'll help you set up everything. I'll put up the money. If you like the place, you and Maudie can have it with a few terms."

"Terms? Like, what terms?"

"I don't want my son raised in a whorehouse, Oney. The bargain is this: I'll get you the ranch. You can take some stock from Twin Oaks to help get you started. You can take the Percherons. Better take the cow, too. I expect you'll need milk for a long time, and take Woody. You never tell him about me until I'm ready. Twin Oaks is too dangerous."

"Well," Oney allowed, "we did have that one shooting."

"Wasn't a shooting, Oney. It was a killing. Bullets flying wild, busting up mirrors. You say *one time*, but how many men were there regularly and armed to the teeth? We just didn't know it. Just tell me, Oney. Does my offer interest you or not?"

"I'm sure you know it does. We love that little baby like he was our own, and a chance for a place that's really ours. I'm sure Maudie would love everything about your bargain. Do you think the house has a kitchen?"

"Let's ride over and see."

–oOo–

As time rolled on, days became months and the months became years. Oney's predictions about the future of the bordello's business proved to be exact. The great herd drives no longer came from Texas and Oklahoma north to meet the railroads. Instead, the railroads had created spur lines south all the way to the Rio Grande, and north to the grasslands of Wyoming and Montana.

Winters had always been slow for the business at Twin Oaks, but now the spring and summer business that was counted on had dwindled to only a visitor or two a week. The biggest surprise of all was the windfall which made up the lost income most generously. The unexpected income was delightfully shocking and came from Israel Greenbaum.

The suit Antoine had sent to the Greenbaum store had impressed Israel so profoundly, he instantly ordered a half dozen more.

"Two in black, small," he ordered, "two black, medium. One large brown and one large blue—a C.O.D. order. Send me the name of your Kansas bank and I will deposit money in a transfer account the same day, I receive the suits in good order."

If the first order was a shock, it was nothing compared to the next order that came two weeks later for a dozen more suits.

"He can't be selling that many suits in his little store. It's mostly a hardware store, anyhow. He sells some work clothes, but suits? What do think's going on here?" Amber asked Antoine.

"I'm as lost as you are. I'll write Pasquale. Maybe he can find out something."

"Pasquale?"

"The bartender at Tracy's. That dive where we first met."

Contacting a snoop like Pasquale proved to be the right thing.

"Look here," Antoine announced, holding a letter of response from his bartender friend. "It seems your friend Israel has become a wholesaler of our product. He's a jobber."

"How?" Amber was incredulous.

"According to Pasquale, he has uncles who own stores in Chicago and New York. Israel buys your suits and resells them to these other stores. He's running a warehouse where merchants can order the suits made here at Twin Oaks."

"Am I supposed to be mad or something about this?" Amber asked.

"Why would you? So, he makes a buck, too. He's giving us some good business. He buys a lot and pays on time. I like the idea."

"Put that way, deal me in! The only problem is we can't fill those kinds of orders. It's just me, Claudia and Mexican Rose. Since Maude left us, Rose also has the kitchen. We need help, Antoine."

A small ad in Tom Prentiss' *Oceola Weekly News* brought an unexpected response. Amber and Antoine were both pleased and unsure. The ad had read:

> *Wanted. Women who are able to sew garments.*
> *Fair pay. Come in person to Twin Oaks Ranch.*
> *West of Town five miles. Old Train Road.*

"We said that we'd pay fair, Amber. Can we do that and hire so many?"

Amber thought a long time. "Well, I think they ought to make what the men do as farm hands or miners. I want to pay what the men make."

"Are you sure about that, Amber? I don't think women earn as much as men."

"They will at Twin Oaks Tailoring! The war took too many men, Antoine, too many women left alone to support whole families. I want them paid well. I think we'll be the ones who profit by it, too."

Four were hired the first day, and two days later, Antoine removed the ad. The bordello commerce was lost forever, but over the next decade the commercial sewing endeavor grew in ways Amber and Antoine had not even considered.

First, of course, was the Greenbaum account. Next, a department store in Chicago wanted to know if shirts could be acquired. Belnap Hardware of Louisville, Kentucky, was searching for a supplier who could provide work garments.

They brought in more sewing machines, and more floor space of the mansion was committed to garment production. The manor became a disorganized, unmanageable maze of stairs, hallways, work areas, and storage spaces. Eventually, the largest of Twin Oaks three barns would be converted to a full-fledged factory, complete with a central heating plant and ceiling fans for hot Kansas summers. Fresh water brought in from the windmill along with the installation of indoor plumbing, although somewhat still experimental, made the sewing plant the most modern building west of Kansas City. The loft of the barn proved an adequate storage place for bolts of cloth, and Charles, with horse and wagon, made daily pick-up and delivery journeys to the Oceola Wells Fargo. He was jokingly referred to as *Twin Oaks Tailoring's One-man Shipping Department.* When the scale of pay became known, a few men applied for work at the sewing center. Antoine politely rejected them. He had misgivings about men being able to sew, but more than that, he had misgivings about how they'd treat the other workers.

Profits were generous, employees were grateful, and Amber was happier than she had ever been. She thought of Charlotte often and wondered if she would be proud of the recent changes at the Oaks. She was confident Charley would rejoice.

Antoine felt good about all things, too. He received letters from Maude telling about the life and times of Woody. Antoine realized his son was no longer an infant but instead, a strapping young lad. Occasionally, Antoine would journey to Haverford by buggy or saddle horse and, from seclusion, would attempt to catch a glimpse of his son. At times, he would watch the farmhouse from hiding for hours, just hoping for a glimpse of

Woody. Antoine would see him at play in the yard, crossing the lane to the barn, or riding his pony.

"For heaven's sake, Antoine. Why don't you just go to him?" Amber asked. Frustrated, she could see no reasoning for Antoine's actions. Antoine longed to see him in the worst way. He wanted to talk with him, and hold him in his arms.

He had things he would have to explain to the boy. How would he tell him about his absence or about his mother? How would he ever explain what kind of a man he was? Would Woodrow understand when he told him he was actually a Mendoza? Would he understand that he was the son of a very wealthy Spanish vintner from a place called Acadia—in Spain, no less? Antoine never once considered Woodrow as adopted. He had decided the boy was of his own blood and never wavered on that resolve. He would tell him all these things. He had to. It could not wait much longer, he thought.

Or then? A haunting thought that burned his brain constantly. Why tell him anything? He was a happy young man. Would knowing his heritage, his mother, her death, and the reason for him being with the Ledbetters instead of his father—would any of these things make him happier or a better man? Antoine had decisions to make. He only hoped he could make the right ones. He vowed he would go to see him, soon—very soon.

Chapter Twenty-eight

Amber arose early on that late summer morning. She was having coffee while sitting in the front porch swing.

A beautiful morning, she thought. *A day like this makes you want to live forever.*

She cast her gaze down the hill to the converted barn. Already a stream of seamstresses was filing through the main door to take up their machines. They were laughing and joking with one another. They seemed so happy and anxious to begin their day.

"How different," she thought. How different from the New Orleans slavery where she, Claudia, and Yvonne had labored so very long ago. She felt good about everything: the morning, the factory, and Mexican Rose's coffee.

And then, just when Amber thought nothing could ever go wrong again in her charmed life, Charles, who had been in town picking up supplies, brought her the worst news she could have imagined.

"Miss Amber! Miss Amber!" Amber knew by the urgency in his voice something was terribly wrong.

"It's the marshall," he said, "Marshall Grady—he was in a gunfight down in the train yard. He's shot bad. He's killed old Billy Whitsell and shot Alton Stewart up. Alton, he might die pretty soon, the doctor said, but Mister Grady; he's shot bad, too. You get yourself ready, Miss Amber. I get us a fresh horse and take you to him."

"Is he dyin'?" Stunned, Amber was doing her best to choke back her tears.

"I get the buggy hooked up to a strong horse and we go see, Miss Amber. We go see."

–oOo–

"Losing an eye is always a serious matter, Miss Juliardo. The wound itself is not so bad and should heal up alright. It looks to me like a bullet must have hit the wood slats in a cattle car. Big splinter of wood hit Grady's eye."

"Will he ever see out of that eye again?" Amber quizzed Doc Pritchard.

"Can't say for sure," the doctor offered. "What I can say for sure is it's gonna be a while. I'm a lot more scared of this here wound in the side of his chest. He's breathin', all ragged like. Could be lung wound. Bullet hole in the right place. Bullet went clear through. Ain't no lead in his chest. So that means if the blood stops—clots up, you know, he ought to be alright. Takes time, though—bedtime— flat on your back time. I'm thinking he's pretty lucky. Lung wounds usually kill right off. The fact he's still alive is right promisin'."

"What was he doing in the train yard in the middle of the night, anyhow?" Amber was both scared and angry.

"His job, Miss Juliardo. Couple of local troublemakers thinkin' they could rob a train! I know both of them. I've sewn them up a time or two. Just local drunks. Old skinny Whitsell—well, Grady killed him right off. Al Stewart probably be dead before nightfall. Going in the dark after that pair—well, I can tell you now, I sure ain't got that kind of stuff. Grady—well, Grady's bold as they come."

"Can I take him home?"

"Not today. Tomorrow maybe. Day after be even better. I'd just as soon he not get all jostled around. Give his blood a chance to clot up good and strong. 'Specially if the lung has been hit."

"Go home, Charles," Amber said. "Tell Claudia what's happening. Come back for me day after tomorrow. Bring the Studebaker buggy. Good springs ought to help him get home with a smooth ride. Rig up something so he can lay flat. Blankets, water—you go now, Charles. Tell Claudia not to come here. Keep the factory going."

For two days, Grady Cole, filled with sleep-inducing laudanum, rested. Fitfully at times, but at least asleep deep enough to avoid the pain of a blinded eye and the shortness of breath accompanying the lesion in his chest. Amber sat quietly at his side, his hand held lightly in her own.

–oOo–

"There's a man here to see you Grady," Amber told him.

Grady lay in the double bed he had shared with Amber in the first-floor bedroom that was now Amber's, but had once belonged to Charlotte and Christof. For ten days now, Amber had brought him his food, changed his bandages, and spoon-fed him laudanum when the eye pain became more than he could tolerate.

"He says his name is Alfred Dunning—uniform and a badge. He's a cop of some kind. Do you know him?"

"Alfred's here? Yeah, I know him. He's my boss."

"Are you up to seeing him? Should I bring him in?"

Grady put his hand to the heavy bandage over his left eye.

"How about a half an ounce, Amber? The eye's smarting some. Half an ounce and then let him in."

Constable Al Dunning entered the bed chamber with a room-lighting smile. A large man, he wore the official grey uniform of the U.S. Marshall's office. He removed his western-styled hat and revealed a mostly bald head. He extended a huge right hand that was much stronger than Grady's.

"Damn, Grady! I'm glad to see you. You had all of us so worried."

"Hello, Al."

"I never thought in a million years I'd call on one of my wounded officers in a whorehouse—don't that just beat all?"

"Ain't been that kind of a house in a long time, Al. We call it *Amber's Place.*"

"I'm guessing Amber is that good-looker that let me in here?"

"You are truly a fine detective, Al. You figured that out right away. And she is a good-looker, isn't she?"

"If I had a chance at one like that, I'd love being shot." Dunning flashed a huge, vulgar grin.

"I'm okay with it."

"Well, I'm here all about good news, Grady."

"And it goes like, what?" Grady asked suspiciously.

"It's like we're going to take you out of the sticks and move you right uptown. We going to take you right off the horse you ride, and give you a padded swivel chair in the Kansas City office right next to mine."

"Why doesn't that smell as good as it sounds?" was Grady's response.

"Look, Grady, I'm not going to kid around with you. You've done a good job out here. We just think you might not be as able as you have been. I'm talking about the fact you've been shot through the lungs and likely you're losing a lamp."

"Maybe not," Grady said.

"Here's the deal I have for you." Al Dunning carefully expanded his story.

"We have more crime in Kansas than we've ever had. We have some good marshalls—like you have been. On the other hand, we have some marshalls just drawing pay. We know if we had you in the city where you could really look things over, see the whole picture all at once. You could help assign the right men to the right jobs."

"I'm not sure I'd like the city, Al. I've been here a long time."

"I didn't want to, but just to save time, here it is. We know you've been here a long time. We also know you spent a lot of time guarding this here— this here, *Amber's Place*—a lot more than you should have. Now, you've been wounded and likely have an eye shot out. I'm offering you the job I described in Kansas City. Either take it, or retire on half pension."

"That's pretty quick, Al. I knew some things were going to change for me. Can I have a day or two to worry on it?"

"I can do better than that, Grady. Take till the first of next month. First day of September either show up at the Kansas City office at nine, or don't. Your call, pal. I'd like a chance to work with you, but it's a big change. You've been a cowboy out here and working in an office will be a change. Hey, who's to say? You might love it. Oh, and if you need more recovery time, just let me know.

–oOo–

"If I'm going to Kansas City, I want to get married," Amber pouted.

"Where's that coming from?" Grady responded.

"We've been sleeping in the same bed every night for nearly ten years now. I think it's time you ask me to marry you."

"Amber, I've asked you to marry me a hundred times. Sure as shooting I'm all for it, but why did you decide right now?"

"Cuz now I'll have a one-eyed husband, and everyone will feel sorry for me. They'll say, 'Poor Amber. She's saddled to that one-eyed fellow from Oceola.' You know—it's like when a man has a one-eyed horse. Folks say, 'poor mister so and so, he's got a one-eyed horse.' Nobody ever says, 'poor horse, you only got one eye.' Or they might say, 'See that man with the eye patch? I'll bet he's a pirate. That lovely girl with him is probably a slave, and he does terrible things to her.'"

Grady couldn't stifle the laughter. "Damn it, Amber. Don't do that. It hurts too much to laugh. It's fine with me. We'll get married, and I promise if the eye does get well, you can put it out again."

"I want to get married in a Catholic church."

"Okay," Grady agreed. "Are you a Catholic?"

"No, but Claudia says they do more at weddings. They ring bells and eat bread and drink wine. Communion, they call it. They do all sorts of things. She says the priest wears a robe instead of a suit and she says they speak Latin."

"I'm sure we can find a nice Catholic church in Kansas City where the priest speaks Latin and wears a robe."

"No, Grady. I want to be married right here. Right in Oceola."

Grady carefully considered his answer to a sore spot. "But, Amber—you told me once you were afraid the ladies in the church would not accept you." Grady was as gentle as he had ever been with this sensitive subject.

"Don't worry me no more, Grady."

"So—what was it that changed your feelings on this matter."

"I don't worry if they like me or not anymore. Most of them work for me. The rest would like to. Hey, you old pirate! Do you feel well enough to try some of those terrible things?"

The next day, they had to face the discomfort of telling Antoine and the others that they would be leaving Twin Oaks.

Chapter Twenty-nine

"Dear Amber," Claudia's letter started:

"The factory is doing well, and I have been managing it along with Antoine. You've been gone six months now and I want to tell you we miss you terribly. How is Grady? I hope he is recovering. We all feel so bad about his eye.

"I felt I should let you know that all Antoine talks about anymore is going to be with his son. He even says he's going to take the boy to Spain. I wanted you to know that, even if he does, I can manage here alright.

"Also, I thought you should know I'm closing the big house. Antoine is in Haverford a good deal of the time near Woody and Oney and Maude. I was living in the house with just Mexican Rose. I'm sure you can't guess what happened. Rose and Charles fell in love and took off for Mexico.

"Antoine has some Indian boys looking after the livestock, and Sally Two Feather and I have moved into the cabin Oney and Maude used.

"We received a new order from the Army to make some shirts. It should pay us well according to Antoine's arithmetic. We have sixty machines

running now. We're making a good deal of money now, but I'm not spending any of it. I know nothing lasts forever and I've been broke before. Your money is here. Write when you want it. Antoine has Vonnie's and is keeping it for Woody.

"I covered the furniture in the big house and just left everything there, except for Mister Willcox Gibbs. I know you love that old machine, and so I brought it here with me. I also brought along our red lantern for old-time's sake. Who knows, I may need it sometime."

Your pal and partner,
Claudia

Amber folded the letter neatly and tucked it into her apron pocket. Over the next few days, she would re-read it many times..

From the red lantern days to a thriving sewing factory. How did all that happen? she thought long and hard. *Claudia was right. Nothing lasts forever.*

–oOo–

"Are you really my father?"

Antoine studied the upturned face before him. It was profusion of freckles, azure-blue eyes, and an aquiline nose with an upturned tip.

A handsome and honest face, Antoine thought as he answered.

"It's true. I am your father. Come to be with you at last."

"You were gone a long time. Maudie said you'd come. I was waiting for you."

"I thought I had good reasons for being away, now I'm not so sure. I am sure though that we're together now, and I want to know all about you."

The boy stood leaning against Maude Ledbetter. He was unsure of this stranger, but confident of the protection offered by the sturdy figure supporting him.

"Nothing to know," the boy said. "I got a pony. Would you like to see her? Her name is Vonnie. Papa Oney said that's my momma's name."

"Yes. It is your mother's name. I haven't said it for a long time. It's a wonderful name for a pony."

"I named her that because I love her. Did you love my mother?"

"With all my heart. After all, she gave me you."

"Can you tell me stories about her? About my mother, I mean."

"We can talk about her. I want you to know how much she loved you. Your mother was very special."

"Papa Oney says she's in heaven now."

"I'm so sure he's right. We have so many things to talk about. I want you to come away with me on a very long trip. We'll have lots of time to talk."

"Where will we go?" the boy wanted to know. "I can't be gone for very long. Papa Oney needs me here at the ranch."

"What is it that you do to help out?"

"Well, I milk the cow. We used to have a cow named Jennifer. She was a Jersey. We got a Holstein now—Martha. She's a big cow. Taller than me. I feed chickens and hunt eggs. Oh, I keep the goats from the garden—that's hard—they're smart."

"He's a real good worker." Maude said. "It'll be hard to be without him for very long."

"I'd better ask Papa."

"We'll be back pretty soon. Your Papa Oney has already said our trip is alright. We'll cross a great ocean. There's a land you need to know about. Some people I want you to see. Some people I want to see you."

"You mean we're gonna go on a boat?" His eyes widened.

"A great ship—a land called Spain—and a town that shares its name with you—Acadia. We'll be on the ship a long time. We can talk and talk. I'll tell you everything about your mother. You can tell *me* about your pony."

–oOo–

It seemed to Amber that she and Grady had just settled themselves in Kansas City when the offer came.

"Look, Amber!" Grady was obviously excited about the letter he held in his hand. "When I heard about this, I sent a letter to them. I never expected to hear back so soon."

"Canada!?" Amber was confused. "You want to go to Canada? We've only been here two years. We just bought this house." She gestured with outstretched arms calling Grady's attention to the lovely cottage setting they had shopped so hard for.

"It's a great opportunity, Amber. Canada's still wild...like Kansas was a hundred years ago. The shopkeepers and lawyers haven't cut it all up yet. It'll be a chance for us to be a part of something. Right from the beginning. Something great. Wild and wonderful."

"So, they want you, they want you for, what?"

"A teacher. I'll be an instructor of American policing techniques to the Royal Mounted Police Force. The Mounties, Amber! They are the lawmen of the wilderness."

Amber thought of Charlotte. How she must have felt when she came to the wilds of early Kansas. Amber admitted to herself she was excited. It was the thought of a new land, a wild and primitive land. It lay ahead of her as wild Kanas had Charlotte. She somehow knew a great and wonderful adventure lay ahead of her and Grady.

–oOo–

Late that night, Grady held Amber tightly in his arms. "Are you upset about this Canada thing?" he asked her in a whisper.

"Not really," she replied. "My place is with you. If you're in Canada, so will I be, Grady. The only problem is you keep moving me further and further north. Are you forgetting I'm a southern belle from New Orleans? Couldn't you find a job in Florida? Mexico, maybe? We just seem to be heading north all the time."

"Amber, do you ever feel bad that we never had any children?" Grady continued in a gentle, intimate way.

"Well, we never tried not to. It's just how things turned out. I'm okay with it," she replied.

"We could adopt a child if you wanted to. That turned out good for Oney and Maude."

"Sure, we could think about adopting a child. That might be a pretty good thing; I just hope it's not an Eskimo."

Epilogue

The county auditor of Haverford County, Kansas, was an overweight, sweaty, little man, who made it a practice to be as unpleasant as he could.

"Look through the records as long as you please," he said. "Just don't ask me any questions. It's all there in black and white and I can't interpret it any way except what's in front of you."

"Well," Willet began, "my wife and I have that old place out on Old Train Road. We inherited it from my father who never told us much about it. Do you have any information about the old place?"

"I'm the auditor. I'm not a historian. I just know what the ledgers say."

"Seems to me the auditor should know about an old place like that," Jennifer interjected. "It's so prominent. That old house, must have been a place of beauty once."

"Not in my day—just an old wreck. The county commissioners keep hoping a tornado will take it. They fear the county might have to take it down someday. They ain't crazy about fronting the money to pay for that, I can tell you."

"Wouldn't they just pass the bill on to me, and I'd be stuck for the cost?" Willett said.

"Old wreck like that—some folks just quit payin' the taxes, and the county gets stuck. Figure it's not worth much to anyone. You might get some answers from old lawyer Pritchard. His family been 'round here forever. He might know some stuff. Ain't nobody lived in that old place since the 1930's, I think. Amos—that's his name, Amos Pritchard. He must have been born in those days. Anyway, he takes a lot of pride in his local knowledge. Calls himself 'the keeper of the keys.' Go see him, and let me get back to work."

-oOo-

"Can't see you today." The voice on the phone's other end sounded old and raspy. "I do want to see you, though. I have some notes my father gave me about the old Twin Oaks place. I need to find them and then I'll talk with you. Could you come about three tomorrow?"

"Three is good," Jennifer answered. "We have heard a lot about you, and we hope you can give us some information about the house on Old Train Road."

"Yeah. Amber's Place."

"Amber's Place?"

"Come at three—we'll talk then." The line went silent.

"Well," Jenifer began, "looks like tomorrow's the day. Here's an idea: let's drive out to the old house and look around. We're free for the afternoon anyway."

It was a twenty minute drive to Old Train Road, and the summer afternoon was a pleasant one. As they drove into the lane, Willett looked up the hill to the house.

"She still looks stately even in her worn-out condition."

"I can only imagine what life must have been like for whoever it was that lived here. I can just picture grand ladies in Paris gowns, handsome, young men in cutaway coats. They probably had wonderful balls here. Concerts, too, I'll bet."

"A grand lifestyle," Willet agreed. The rest of the afternoon was given over to their active imaginations as they explored the grounds and the old cemetery.

"Here's a tombstone—says 'Randall Big Turtle.' Would you think he was a native American?" Jennifer asked. Willet nodded. Lost in thought they wandered on. They decided not to attempt to enter the house. Decrepit porches and missing entrance planks made it look risky.

"I guess selling it is the right thing to do." Willett was dismayed by the condition. Without answering, head lowered in disappointment, Jennifer led the way back to their Buick.

The wait was a long one. Willet thought three o'clock would never come. The visit to the property had whetted their appetites for information.

"It's like walking back into history," Jennifer said. "Those were our ancestors who lived there, and we know nothing about them."

"I only saw the name Acadia on two of those tombstones."

"I saw them," Jennifer said. "Ansel Acadia and Ida Mae. Ansel's is such a small stone. Would you think a child, maybe?"

–oOo–

Adam Pritchard proved to be just as accommodating and charming as the county auditor was not.

"Come in. Please sit. I'll have Reuben bring coffee in a moment."

The house was an old one decorated in the style of the 1930's. Oriental carpets throughout—settees and rockers—ladder-back chairs and an art deco-styled gaming table made up the décor.

"I wish I had more to tell you. That old place has fascinated me for years."

Jennifer examined the old man in front of her closely. *He looks like a judge,* she thought. Indeed, he was old but rigid in his posture, and he was perfectly groomed in his navy pinstripe and paisley tie.

"There's a few old newspaper clippings I found. My father and my grandfather, both doctors, were fascinated by Twin Oaks, too. Here's an article about a bandit who was shot on that property by a federal marshall, and another about a woman named Yvonne Acadia—same name as yours. Seems she drowned somehow. When I was a boy, there was an old windmill out there—a big cattle tank, too. Might be she drowned in that old tank."

"We saw no windmill," Jennifer said.

"I know," the old man responded. "Tornado of '39 took it down. Once it was on the ground, folks who needed some lumber just packed it away piece at a time."

"A lot of planking from the porches is missing, too. Is that what happened to them?" Willett said.

They took a necessary break while the servant Reuben served the coffee.

"I 'spect so. Old house just seemed so deserted; folks didn't even realize they were stealing. My father told me that at one time the old place was fully furnished. The depression comes along. Folks hurting so bad they just took all of it. Sold it for a little cash, I'd guess. In fact, before the depression there was a factory there."

"A factory?" Jennifer asked.

"Sure enough was. Lots of women working there making clothes for the army—department stores, too. Depression comes along, sudden like, all's gone. Man named Woodrow Acadia was running the place. When it went under, he went back to a farm he owned over in Haverford. He lived there till he died sometime in the early 1940s, after the outbreak of World War II. He and his wife are in that old cemetery. Ida Mae, she was."

"When I called you yesterday, you referred to the property as Amber's Place. What was that about?" Jennifer asked.

"I surely don't know. My father told me that was the way folks had always called that place. No one knows why. It's like the name, Willcox Gibbs. I can't find anyone in the census by that name. Still, it's somehow tied to that tract."

"What happened to the women who used to work there? What did they do?"

"They did what women always do—they adapted. For Christ's sake, if the dinosaurs could adapt like women, they'd still be here."

On that note, Willet and Jennifer thanked the old lawyer for all his help and departed his office.

"I'm in favor of selling," Willett told Jennifer. "I have a good job, but we don't really have the kind of money it would take to rehab that old place."

"I know," Jennifer responded. "But it's nice to dream about it. Can you imagine what it was like to live there in its heyday? Beautiful ladies–all the elegance in the world–I'll bet they never had a single problem in their entire lives. I know we need to sell it, though."

"We need a new car," Willett said, "and if we're ever going to start a family, we need to get going."

"Well, you know where the motor is. All you have to do is start it up."

"I've got a call or two to make, and then I'll call the buyers."

–oOo–

Rob Ashby stood quietly before the door of his superior, J.L. Hawkins.

"Mister Hawkins will see you now, Rob," his secretary said. "Just go right in."

The two men exchanged greetings with a handshake. Ashby opened the conversation.

"That Oceola deal with the Acadias is about set."

"Any concessions to our original offer?"

"Just a couple. You might recall that an old house is a burden on the site. The owners have worked it out with the local fire department to take it down with a training burn. We get the cleanup, but we'll salvage enough chimney and fireplace brick to pay for most of it."

"Sounds okay. What else?"

"We offered two. They have countered at two twenty-five and they get to name one of the streets."

"Try to do it at two-ten, two-fifteen maybe. Anyway, if they won't ease up, go ahead with two and a quarter. I like the location. Let's make it work. Oh, by the way, what do they want to name the street? Not something stupid, I hope."

"No. *Amber's Place.*"

"*Amber's Place?*"

"Yep."

"Sounds good to me, close the deal."

Acknowledgements

After telling the story of Amber, it's necessary to thank a few friends who provided invaluable help along the way: Barb Northup for her assistance with the story, and Pat Tomazic who did the initial editing. I also owe a debt to my writing associates, who encouraged me every step of the way: Cary, Jerry, Nancy, and Rob, who are with me in a writers' group. Finally, I want to thank the wonderful folks at Drinian Press, LLC.

Most especially I'd like to thank my wife of fifty years for her unending love and support. I'm pleased to dedicate this story to her.

Gary Harmon

About the Author

Born and raised in Southern Indiana, Gary Harmon's young life was filled with the daily handling of horses and cattle. His family operated a large stockyard where the daily trading, buying, and selling of livestock were his earliest memories. After Gary's discharge from the U.S. Army, he was employed as a buyer of hogs, cattle, and occasionally, sheep for one of the nation's major meat packing companies of that time. A second career in real estate brought about a love for historic houses and the classic architecture of eons long gone.

Strong storytelling and attention to detail are characteristics of his writing. This fact is no less true in *Amber's Place* than it was in his first novel, *The Broken Spur*.